ROAD TO NOWHERE

Joe slammed his foot down on the kick starter, and the dirt bike roared. He motioned to Gina, and she hopped on behind him. The engine screamed as Joe raced toward the oncoming Jeep. At the last second, he swerved to veer past the Jeep, turning onto a rutted trail that disappeared in the trees.

"Are they still following us?" he yelled.

"Yes!" Gina told him. "And they're gaining!"

Now Joe knew he was going to have to push the bike to the limit. He crouched low over the handlebars and leaned hard into a sharp turn.

"Look out!" Gina screamed as they came out of the curve.

Joe's head reared back, and he slammed on the brakes when he saw a second Jeep blocking the trail. Two men wearing camouflage jumpsuits stood in front of the Jeep. The submachine guns in their hands told Joe this was the end of the line.

Books in THE HARDY BOYS CASEFILES® Series

Available from ARCHWAY Paperbacks

THE HARDY BOYS CASEFILES

No. 77

RING OF EVIL 2

SURVIVAL RUN

FRANKLIN W. DIXON

EAU CLAIRE DISTRICT LIBRARY

AN ARCHWAY PAPERBACK
Published by POCKET BOOKS
New York   London   Toronto   Sydney   Tokyo   Singapore

86613

The sale of this book without its cover is unauthorized. If you purchased this book without a cover, you should be aware that it was reported to the publisher as "unsold and destroyed." Neither the author nor the publisher has received payment for the sale of this "stripped book."

This book is a work of fiction. Names, characters, places and incidents are either the product of the author's imagination or are used fictitiously. Any resemblance to actual events or locales or persons, living or dead, is entirely coincidental.

AN ARCHWAY PAPERBACK *Original*

An Archway Paperback published by
POCKET BOOKS, a division of Simon & Schuster Inc.
1230 Avenue of the Americas, New York, NY 10020

Copyright © 1993 by Simon & Schuster Inc.
Produced by Mega-Books of New York, Inc.

All rights reserved, including the right to reproduce this book or portions thereof in any form whatsoever. For information address Pocket Books, 1230 Avenue of the Americas, New York, NY 10020

ISBN: 0-671-79461-2

First Archway Paperback printing July 1993

10 9 8 7 6 5 4 3 2 1

THE HARDY BOYS, AN ARCHWAY PAPERBACK
and colophon are registered trademarks of Simon & Schuster Inc.

THE HARDY BOYS CASEFILES is a trademark
of Simon & Schuster Inc.

Cover art by Brian Kotzky

Printed in the U.S.A.

IL 6+

Chapter

1

"I'VE BEEN GIVING this case some serious thought," Joe Hardy said, "and I still have one question." He pushed his cup of cold coffee away and slid down low in the booth. "I hate coffee," he muttered. "Why did I order it?"

A faint smile crossed his brother Frank's lips. "Is that the big question?"

Seventeen-year-old Joe rolled his blue eyes toward the ceiling but didn't find anything worth checking out there. "No, that's not it. I was just wondering. We worked as baggage handlers for almost a week until we were let go, and I want to know if we're going to be paid for that time."

"The job was just a cover, you know that," his brother, who was a year older, reminded him. Frank's gaze wandered to the window that looked out on the interior of the sprawling airport terminal. No doubt about it, Atlanta's Hartsfield Airport was big. Thousands of people passed through it every day, bound for thousands of places. The last time Frank had sat in this same coffee shop with his brother, he had seen the mysterious Gray Man—an important member of a secret government agency known simply as the Network—prowling the wide corridors. Now Frank didn't see much beyond the reflection of his own brown hair and eyes.

"I know that," Joe said with a sigh, brushing a lock of blond hair off his forehead. "But I think we should have gotten paid for lugging all those suitcases around."

"Could we deal with that later?" a third voice chimed in. This one belonged to Gina Abend, a check-in clerk for Eddings Air, who was sitting next to Frank. "What I want to know is—what do we do now?"

Joe checked out her enormous green eyes and blond curly hair and knew that she was the best thing he had set eyes on all week.

"When in doubt, the best place to start is with a review of the facts," Frank suggested.

"We know that Solomon Mapes was running a luggage theft ring, and that he got mixed up with an international terrorist group somehow. They then killed him, probably to silence him." Frank observed Gina's reaction. He knew that this rehash was hard for her because she had been in love with Mapes. She seemed to be holding up all right, though.

Michael Eddings, the president and founder of Eddings Air, had hired the Hardys to investigate a growing problem with luggage theft at the airline's main hub in Atlanta. Working undercover as baggage handlers, Frank and Joe had discovered that the leader of the luggage theft ring was Solomon Mapes, a pilot for Eddings Air.

The case had had its share of twists and turns. Frank was used to that. This case had one twist, though, that Frank couldn't unravel. Just as the Hardys were closing in on Mapes, he had been brutally murdered while Frank and Gina watched helplessly.

"Tell me more about these terrorists," Gina said, her voice detached, almost cold. "The Assassins? Is that right?"

Joe nodded. "Yes." He knew what Gina was going through because the first time the Hardys had run into the Assassins, Joe's girlfriend, Iola Morton, had been killed by a car

3

bomb. At the time the only way he could deal with it was to shut down his emotions and concentrate on nailing the killers.

"Sometimes the Assassins work for the highest bidder," Joe explained. "Sometimes I think they just kill people for the fun of it."

Gina frowned as she picked at the salad on her plate. "I don't get it. I know Solomon wasn't a saint, but I don't know why he'd be involved with terrorists."

"The Gray Man told us the Assassins were using Solomon's luggage theft ring to smuggle things around the country," Frank said.

"You don't sound convinced," Gina noted.

"I'm not," Frank replied. "The Assassins run a very tight operation. I don't know why they'd want a bunch of small-time thieves involved."

"Do you think the Gray Man lied to you?" Gina asked.

"It wouldn't be the first time," Joe commented. "The Network operates on a need-to-know basis. If they decide you don't need to know, they don't tell you."

"There are two things that still bother me about this case," Frank said. "First, why did the head of security for Eddings Air sabotage the private jet of the founder and president of the company?"

"I wouldn't waste a whole lot of time on that one," Joe grumbled. "Hank Forrester seems determined to take that secret to jail with him."

"Maybe we'll find the answer to it while we're solving the other riddle that's been on my mind," Frank said. He waited until he was sure he had both Joe's and Gina's full attention. "Just before the Assassins killed Mapes and took off, they grabbed a tube-shaped leather fishing rod case.

"Maybe they didn't want to leave empty-handed," Joe suggested.

Frank shook his head. "They opened the case and checked inside first. There was something in it that they wanted, and I think it's the key to whatever is going on with the Assassins and the Network. I want to know what it is."

"If it will lead us to Solomon's killers," Gina said, "then I want to know, too."

"Let's get started," Joe said. He took one last sip of his coffee, made a face, and stood up. "You pay the bill," he told his brother. "I'll leave the tip."

Joe stuck his hand in his pants pocket to dig out some change and came up with something else instead. "What's this?" he muttered as he pulled out a torn strip of heavy paper.

"You're just full of deep questions today, aren't you?" Frank responded. "Why did I order coffee? Are we going to get paid? What's in my pocket?"

Joe ignored Frank and studied the ripped band of paper. On one side what looked like part of a name was handwritten. Joe flipped the paper strip over, and his eyes widened as he stared at what was left of the blue Eddings Air logo.

"Gina," he said. "What do you do if a passenger checks a bag that doesn't have any ID tags?"

Gina smiled at him. "What is this? A test of my check-in clerk training?"

Joe smiled back. "Some airlines ask passengers to fill out temporary ID tags, which they then attach to the bags. The tags are usually just paper bands with the airline's logo printed on them. Does Eddings Air do anything like that?"

"Sure," Gina said. "It's standard procedure. Why?"

Joe's smile widened as he put the scrap of paper on the table. "I think I just found our first clue in tracking down the mysterious leather fishing rod case. I must have ripped that off without realizing it when I crashed into that Assassin in the storage room. Remember?"

Frank nodded. "You did run right into the guy who was carrying the case." He looked at his brother. "I can understand how you might have torn the tag loose during the scuffle—but how did it get in your pocket?"

Joe shrugged. "I don't know. Sometimes I do weird things when people are shooting at me."

"Remind me to go through all your pants pockets when we get home," Frank said. "Maybe I'll find important clues to unsolved cases."

"We don't have any unsolved cases," Joe countered. "You're just jealous because I found a clue."

"I'm suspicious because you realized it *was* a clue," Frank retorted.

"Why don't I just leave while you two beat each other up?" Gina interjected. She picked up the torn tag and squinted at it. "When you're finished playing king of the mountain, we can figure out who this Nikolai Stavrsomething is."

Frank's eyes shifted to Gina. "There's a name on the tag?"

"Yes," she replied. "Well, part of one, anyway." She showed Frank the scrap of paper. "See? There's the first name, *Nikolai*. And

7

THE HARDY BOYS CASEFILES

there's part of the last name. S-t-a-v-r. The rest is missing."

"Let's hope it's enough," Frank said.

"Enough for what?" Joe asked.

"Enough for the computer to tell us who it is," Frank answered.

They both looked at Gina.

"I don't know," she said. "I guess we could check the passenger lists for the past few weeks to see what comes up. But that's a lot of names. It could take a while."

"There might be an easier way," Frank said. "If the case was reported missing by the owner, it should show up in the lost luggage data base that Forrester told us about. We'll still have to search for names that start with those five letters—but there should be fewer of them, and they'll all be in one place."

"I don't know anything about tracing lost luggage," Gina responded. "I just check bags *in*. I don't check them out."

"Don't worry about that," Joe said confidently. "We just need your password to get into the system. Frank can handle it from there."

"Okay," Gina replied. "All we need is a computer terminal."

Frank thought about it for a minute and

then grinned. "I think I know where we can find one to use.

A few minutes later Frank was tapping away on a computer keyboard in a private office.

"Even if Hank Forrester makes bail, I doubt he'll show up here," Joe commented while Frank worked. "Too bad we don't have his personal password. As the Eddings Air security chief, I'll bet he had access to a lot of interesting files."

"The only thing I'm interested in right now," Frank replied as he waited for the screen display to change, "is who that leather case belongs to."

"I hope you guys know what you're doing," Gina said nervously, her eyes darting to the door. "Nobody gave us permission to use this office."

"Nobody said we couldn't, either," Joe responded casually.

"We won't be here long, anyway," Frank said as he studied the data on the monitor. "I think I've got it."

Joe moved around the desk to check the computer screen. "What did you find?"

"Dr. Nikolai Stavrogin reported a fly-fishing rod case missing two weeks ago," Frank answered. "It matches the description of the case the Assassins took."

Joe frowned. "Two *weeks* ago? The case just showed up here two days ago. Why did it take so long to get to Atlanta?"

"Maybe we should ask Dr. Stavrogin," Frank said. He took a notepad out of his pocket and started writing. "His home address is in Washington, D.C., and there's a phone number listed, too. Let's give him a call."

Frank picked up the phone on Forrester's desk and punched in the number. After two rings there was a faint click on the line and a heavily accented voice said, "Hello. This is Nikolai Stavrogin. I am not here now. I have gone fishing. If you have urgent business, leave a message with my assistant, Denise Wallner, in the Georgetown University physics department." The message gave the telephone number, which Frank quickly jotted down.

"He's on vacation," Frank said, and hung up the phone. "Let's see if the computer can tell us where he went." His fingers moved across the keyboard. "Here it is. He flew to Anchorage, Alaska, and caught a connecting flight to Fairbanks."

"Any address or phone number in Fairbanks?" Joe asked hopefully.

Frank shook his head. "I can't find one, but maybe I'm not looking in the right place." He tapped a few more keys.

Just then the office door flew open and was smashed against the wall. Frank raised his head and sucked in his breath at the sight of two deadly gun barrels aimed at them.

Chapter

2

JOE GRABBED Gina and dragged her down behind the desk. The guys holding the guns looked like cops, but Joe wasn't taking any chances. They might be Assassins dressed in phony police uniforms.

Frank's mind was racing, too, as he pushed his chair away from the desk and dived to the floor. He knew the desk wouldn't protect them for long—a bullet from a powerful handgun would punch through the wood without even slowing down. They had only a few seconds to plan their next move, and Frank frantically tried to think of what it should be.

"Freeze!" a harsh voice barked. "Police!"

Frank cautiously peered out from behind

the desk and saw two pairs of legs clad in the black uniform pants of the Atlanta police. "Don't shoot!" he called out. "We're not armed!"

"Come out with your hands up!" a voice ordered. Frank didn't like the sound of the voice. It was full of nervous tension. Nervous people made mistakes, and Frank definitely did not want to be on the receiving end of any mistake involving weapons that put large holes in people.

"Okay," Frank said, slowly raising his hands above the desk and waving them in the air. "See? I'm not holding anything. I'm going to stand up now."

One at a time Frank, Joe, and Gina came out from behind the desk, holding their hands in the air.

"This is all a misunderstanding," Joe said as one of the officers whirled him around and cuffed his hands behind his back. "There's a simple explanation."

"I'm eager to hear it," a familiar voice replied.

Joe saw Michael Eddings, president and founder of Eddings Air, the man who had hired the Hardys to uncover the luggage theft operation.

*   *   *

EAU CLAIRE DISTRICT LIBRARY

Eddings kept the Hardys and Gina waiting outside his private office for over half an hour before his secretary told them they could go in. As they walked into the office, Eddings murmured something into the telephone, put down the receiver, and leveled an even gaze at the Hardys.

"I'm sorry about the . . . misunderstanding with the police. I heard someone in Forrester's office and didn't want to take any chances. I'm still a little rattled by Solomon Mapes's murder. All this business with the Assassins and the Network—I didn't expect to get involved in an international conspiracy."

"We understand," Frank said. "I'm sure we'll all breathe a lot easier when this case is over."

Eddings's eyes focused on Frank. "This case *is* over. With Mapes dead and Forrester behind bars, the luggage theft ring is out of business."

"That's just the tip of the iceberg," Joe protested. "There's a lot more going on here."

"I don't care," Eddings snapped. "Your father assured me that you boys wouldn't get involved in anything dangerous. Instead, you almost got yourselves killed!" He paused and took a deep breath. "Anyway," he began more calmly, "whatever else may be going

14

on, there's nothing you're going to do about it. You two are officially off the case. I believe I told you that earlier. Well, now I'm putting you on the next flight back to New York.''

"You can't do that!" Joe exclaimed.

"Yes, I can," Eddings replied sharply. "Your plane takes off in fifteen minutes. I've sent someone to pick up your bags. They'll be on the next flight. They may even get to New York before you do. I'm sorry I couldn't put you on a nonstop flight, but I wanted you out of Atlanta, before you could get into any more trouble. So you'll just have to put up with a brief stop in Washington.''

"Washington, D.C.?" Frank responded. His tone was casual, but his brain was on full alert.

"Yes," Eddings said, glancing at his watch. "You should get going. I'll have one of my security guards escort you to the gate. We wouldn't want you to miss that plane, would we?''

"Don't worry," Frank said with a smile as he stood up. "We wouldn't miss it for the world.''

Gina walked to the departure gate with them. "This is kind of an awkward way to say goodbye," she said, glancing back at the guard who was following them from a polite distance. "I guess we'll never know what the Assassins were after."

"Well," Frank responded, "you're half right, anyway. This *is* an awkward way and place to say goodbye." He leaned closer to her. "But Joe and I are still on the case," he added in a whisper.

Gina was obviously puzzled. "What do you mean? Eddings just fired you."

Joe chuckled. "Getting fired never stopped us before." He had seen the light in his brother's eyes when Eddings told them about the extra stop their flight was going to make. "And we never said anything about going home. We only agreed to get on the plane."

Gina's gaze shifted between the two brothers. "I get it. The flight makes a stop in Washington, and that's where Stavrogin lives."

Frank nodded. "That's right."

"Then I'll take the next flight and meet you there," Gina said.

Frank put his hand on Gina's shoulder. "You've been a great help, but—"

Gina brushed his hand away. "But what?" she snapped. "This means a lot more to me than it does to you."

"I know," Frank replied softly. "Try to understand. One of our advantages is that we look like just a couple of average teenagers.

If you were with us, people would notice us more."

"You mean I'd be in the way," Gina said flatly. "I guess you're right," she said after a long pause. "Just promise you'll call me if you find out anything about Solomon's killers."

Joe held his left hand up, his right on his heart. "We promise," he said solemnly.

Gina punched him in the shoulder. "This is serious," she protested.

"Don't waste your time," Frank told her. "The word *serious* isn't in Joe's vocabulary."

The flight to New York was uneventful— except that the Hardys got off in Washington and "forgot" to get back on. A cab ride and a short walk later, Joe and Frank were outside Dr. Stavrogin's office at the Georgetown University physics department. Frank knocked on the door and was mildly surprised when he got a response.

"Come on in," a voice called out. "It's open."

Frank opened the door and found himself staring at a cramped cubicle cluttered with papers and stacks of books. A blackboard covered one wall, and cryptic equations covered the blackboard.

"If you're looking for Dr. Stavrogin, you'll

have to come back. He's on vacation." A young woman's head appeared from behind the single desk in the room. "Don't ever drop anything on the floor in here," she said with a wry grin, running a hand through her tousled red hair. "It'll take you a week to find it."

Joe cleared his throat. "Are you Denise Wallner, Dr. Stavrogin's assistant?" he asked.

"It's hard to assist somebody if you can't find him," she answered. "Dr. Stavrogin took off on a fishing trip to Alaska two weeks ago, and that's the last I heard from him."

"Is there any way to get in touch with him?" Frank asked.

Denise shook her head. "He has a cabin in the middle of nowhere, and there's no phone. He told me he'd call in once a week when he went to town to pick up supplies, but he hasn't called yet. I'm starting to get a little worried."

Frank studied Denise closely for a moment and decided to take a chance. "What I'm about to tell you may sound unbelievable, but please try to believe it. Dr. Stavrogin's life may depend on it."

When Frank finished telling Denise about the Network and the Assassins and the leather case, she only stared at him silently.

18

"Do you have any idea what these terrorists might want with Dr. Stavrogin?" Frank asked.

"I'm afraid I do," Denise Wallner replied in a measured tone that reflected her concern. "But I'm not at liberty to discuss it."

"We know Dr. Stavrogin went to Fairbanks," Joe said. "Could you tell us where his cabin is?"

"It's about an hour north of Fairbanks," she said. "Outside a small town called Big Bear."

Joe turned to Frank. "I hear Alaska is beautiful this time of year."

"I guess we'll have to go to find out for ourselves," Frank said, smiling at Denise. "Thanks for the address."

They left the building and started across the campus. "We'll probably have to leave the campus to find a cab," Frank remarked.

"No, we won't," Joe responded, breaking into a jog and waving a hand in the air. "Taxi!" he shouted.

"We're going to the airport," Joe told the driver as he and Frank got in.

The driver grunted, and the cab lurched away from the curb.

"I guess we lucked out," Frank said to the driver. "I didn't think we'd find a cab on campus. Did you just drop somebody off?"

19

The driver's only reply was to reach behind him and slide the Plexiglas window shut between the front seat and backseat.

"Not very friendly, is he?" Joe remarked.

"At least he's not a talker," Frank said. From the backseat he couldn't get a very good look at the driver, except for his curly black hair.

Frank's eyes shifted to the license on the dashboard. He studied the driver again and leaned over to his brother. "Is it my imagination, or is the guy in the picture a lot fatter than the guy behind the wheel?"

"Maybe he lost weight," Joe suggested.

"You're probably right," Frank said uneasily as the cab sped across the Francis Scott Key bridge and onto the George Washington Memorial Parkway.

That was when Frank realized what was bothering him. "Hey!" he shouted, rapping on the Plexiglas window. "Don't you want to know which airport we're going to?"

Joe frowned. "Is there more than one?"

"Yes!" Frank responded frantically, pounding on the plastic barrier that separated them from the driver. "Washington National and Dulles. How did he know which one we were going to?"

The cab swerved onto an exit ramp, and the tires screamed into a tight turn.

"Maybe he's new in town," Joe offered lamely. "Maybe he didn't know."

"Maybe he doesn't read English, either," Frank said as the cab smashed through a wooden barrier with a sign that announced Bridge Closed for Repairs.

Joe's hands pawed at the seat cushions.

"What are you doing?" Frank snapped.

"Looking for the seat belts," Joe snapped back.

A cluster of construction workers scattered as the cab whisked past them. Joe's hands stopped moving and dug into the seat cushion as the cab plowed through another barrier and rocketed toward a wide gap in the guardrail. A workman with a blowtorch dived out of the way as the cab soared up through the breach.

"We're in trouble!" Frank yelled to his brother, grabbing his arm.

Joe didn't have a chance to answer. His stomach jumped into his throat as the bridge fell away and the dark blue Potomac rushed up to meet them.

Chapter

3

THE CAB HIT the water with a violent jolt, pitching Joe out of his seat. His head smacked into the Plexiglas divider, and the world started to go gray. Sheer willpower kept him from blacking out. He knew the cab would be his coffin if he passed out right then. They weren't underwater yet, but they were getting there fast. He shook his head to try to clear it and checked for his brother.

"Get off me!" Frank groaned.

Joe saw then that he was sprawled on top of Frank. "We've got to get out of here," he said as he untangled himself from his brother. Water was rushing in around the edges of the door frames. It was already ankle deep, and it was cold. Joe tried to open one door, but it was jammed shut. He put his shoulder against it and started to shove.

"Don't do that!" Frank snapped, grabbing Joe's arm and jerking him away from the door. "You probably couldn't open it anyway because of the water pressure. But if you could, we'd get trapped by a wall of incoming water, and the cab would sink like a rock with us still in it."

"We're sinking now!" Joe shot back, eyeing the rising water level in the cab.

"I know," Frank said. "We have to wait until the water comes in almost all the way to the top. Then we take a deep breath from the last bit of air and roll down the window or open the door.

"Wait a minute," Joe said, pointing to the driver slumped over the steering wheel. "What about him?" He tried to open the sliding divider, but it was locked or jammed. He pounded his fist against the hard, clear plastic barrier. "Hey! Wake up in there!"

"That's no good," Frank said. "He's out cold."

"He sure picked a great time to take a nap," Joe muttered, leaning back in the seat. He swung his feet up and smashed his shoes into the Plexiglas. The bottom of the divider popped loose.

Working together, the Hardys pried the divider up enough for Frank to haul the unconscious driver out over the back of the seat. When the water reached the proper level, Joe rolled down the window and swam out. Treading water, he took the driver's limp body from his brother. Finally Frank scrambled out of the sinking wreck, too.

The river continued to fill the cab as it slid to the bottom of the Potomac. The gurgling noise of the rushing water sounded like a grim chuckle as the dark river claimed the doomed cab. A few strong, steady strokes took Frank away from the swirling vortex.

"What now?" Joe panted, struggling to keep his head and the inert cabdriver's above water.

Frank reached out to help his brother with the heavy burden and felt something slap against the side of his face. As he started to brush it away, he saw it was a rope. Looking up, he saw several construction workers in orange hard hats peering down from the bridge that arced overhead.

"Grab the line!" one of them shouted. "We'll pull you up!"

Frank and Joe tied the rope around the cabdriver's chest, and the workers pulled him up and out of the river. When the line came back down, Frank insisted that Joe go next.

Two pairs of strong hands grasped Joe as he clambered onto the bridge. A brawny, bearded guy tried to lead him away from the edge, but Joe wouldn't budge. He shook himself free, got down on his hands and knees, and watched intently as the construction workers threw the line down to Frank. When Frank reached the bridge, the first pair of hands to pull him to safety belonged to Joe.

Frank gave his brother a weak smile, which quickly faded. "Where's the cabdriver?" he asked, alarmed. He grabbed one of the construction workers. "What happened to the guy with the dark, curly hair? He was unconscious when you pulled him out of the water."

"Your friend woke up and took off," another worker answered. He leaned over, rubbing his knee. "He was acting kind of crazy. I told him he should wait for the ambulance so the paramedics could check him out. I even tried to hold him. I figured he was a little delirious. He gave me a kick in the leg that I didn't see coming, and then he was gone."

A siren wailed nearby, and an ambulance rumbled onto the bridge, followed by a police car.

A paramedic jumped out of the ambulance and put a bandage on Joe's forehead while Frank spoke to the two police officers. Frank was convinced the missing driver was an Assassin but didn't mention that to the police. Instead, he stuck to the details of the deadly cab ride.

By the time the officers had finished their questioning, the Hardys' clothes were much dryer. The paramedic said the bump on Joe's head wasn't serious, so the boys decided to head for the airport. One of the construction workers offered to give them a ride.

When they were finally alone in the airport, Frank and Joe talked about the things that had been left unsaid in their conversation with the police.

"That was no accident," Joe muttered as they waited in the ticket line. "That cabdriver wanted to kill us. I'll bet he was an Assassin."

Frank nodded. He knew it was more than possible that an Assassin would sacrifice his own life to complete a murder mission. The terrorists were hardcore fanatics, loyal to the death. "We must be close to something big."

"Brilliant deduction. The only question is, what?"

"There's only one way to find out," Frank said. He stepped up to the ticket counter and handed the clerk a credit card. "Two tickets to Fairbanks, Alaska, please."

The last leg of the flight to Fairbanks was a condensed course in Alaskan history and geography. Frank absorbed every word of the talkative pilot's friendly lecture over the intercom. As they passed over the Alaska Range in the vast wilderness of Denali National Park, the pilot pointed out Mount McKinley off to the west. Even from a great distance the white-capped peak was stunning, rising almost four miles into the crystal-clear air.

For Joe the highlight of the trip came after the plane was on the ground and they were inside the airport terminal. "Look at that!" he marveled, pointing to an old biplane hanging from the ceiling. "How would you like to tour Alaska from the cockpit of one of those?"

"We'll have to settle for a cheap rental car," Frank said.

But they ran into their first obstacle when they tried to rent a car.

"There isn't anything on four wheels available within a two-hundred-mile radius," Frank said as he trudged back from the car-rental booths.

"Let's take a cab into town," Joe suggested. "Maybe we can buy a cheap used car."

Frank stared at his brother. *"Buy* a car?"

"It would have to be a really cheap one," Joe responded. "It's worth a try."

"Okay," Frank relented. "The Assassins are up to something, and a college professor has vanished. What choice do we have?"

They walked out of the terminal to find a cab. Joe saw one in the distance and stepped off the curb to flag it down. But as the cab pulled up, a large motor home rumbled past and suddenly swerved in front of the cab, bearing down on Joe with its horn blaring.

Joe leapt back onto the curb, and the motor home screeched to a halt. The side door swung open, and Joe heard a familiar voice.

"Get in," the voice ordered.

Frank and Joe glanced at each other.

"What are you waiting for?" the voice demanded. "If you don't get in right now, you're going to be sorry you ever came to Alaska."

Chapter

4

FRANK GLANCED inside the motor home, then over at his brother and smiled. "I think we'd better do what she says."

"I agree. She sounds tough," Joe responded as he and Frank got in.

"Hold on," the driver said as the motor home lurched forward. "I haven't got the hang of this yet."

"And just what are you doing here, Gina?" Joe asked.

Gina gave him a quick smile.

"I think we know the answer to that," Frank called out over the rumble of the engine and the chorus of rattles and clanks. The motor home might have resembled a small house inside, but it sounded like a truck full of loose bowling pins. "But how did you find us?"

"Simple," Gina replied. "A friend of mine works in reservations at Eddings Air. Most airlines are tied into a central computerized reservation system. She just told the computer to search for your names, and then she gave me a call when you popped up with reservations to Anchorage and Fairbanks."

"That doesn't explain how you managed to be here waiting for us," Frank pointed out.

Gina laughed. "I figured I'd check for you in town first."

"What if we hadn't been here?" Frank asked her.

Deadly serious now, Gina replied, "Then I would have gone after Solomon's killers by myself."

Joe wandered back to the galley and opened the refrigerator. "We could use some food," he said glumly, staring at the empty shelves.

"You're right," Frank replied. "We need supplies—and not just food. We need clothes, too."

Joe slapped his forehead. "That's right! Our luggage is in New York by now."

"The kind of stuff we need here isn't in our suitcases, anyway," Frank said. "We packed for Atlanta, not Alaska." He paused to make a mental checklist. "We need coats, hats, blankets, maybe gloves."

"Gloves?" Joe responded. "It's the middle of summer!"

"And this is Fairbanks, Alaska," Frank retorted. "We're only a hundred miles from the Arctic Circle. The nights may be short this time of year, but they can get very cold."

Something outside caught Joe's eye. "Hey, look!" he exclaimed. "Used dirt bikes!" He pointed to a sign in front of a motorcycle dealership. "Let's find out how much they cost."

Frank groaned. "Whatever they cost, we can't afford them."

Joe pulled his wallet out and flashed his credit card. "We can't afford to be caught unprepared," he insisted. "If we have to travel in this dinosaur, we need an emergency escape plan."

Two dirt bikes and several mini-malls later, the motor home lumbered out of Fairbanks north on the Steese Highway. Joe was driving, Frank was navigating from the passenger seat, and Gina was resting in back.

"We turn off here to get to Big Bear," Frank said, his eyes moving from a road sign to the map in his lap and back again. "We go north on the Elliot Highway."

"Some highway," Joe grumbled when the pavement gave way to gravel a few miles up the road.

"Get used to it," Frank told him. "Half the roads in Alaska aren't paved, and they're all called highways. Even if the road isn't the greatest, the view sure is."

For the first fifty miles or so, huge southbound semitrailers roared by every few minutes, kicking up clouds of dust, but closer to Big Bear most of the traffic disappeared.

Frank studied the map again as they rolled to a stop at an intersection with another gravel road. There was a gas station on one corner, a café on another, a general store on the third, and a For Sale sign on the fourth.

"We should be close to Big Bear," he said.

"I think this *is* Big Bear," Gina replied from the couch, pointing out the window at a weathered wooden sign above the general store.

Joe grinned when he saw the sign. "Somebody around here has a great sense of humor."

"Big Bear Mini-Mall," Frank read out loud. "Let's see if anybody in the mall can tell us how to find Dr. Stavrogin's cabin."

The only person in the old wood frame

building was a gray-haired woman who came out from behind the counter to greet them. "Howdy," she said cheerfully. "I'm Beth Truman. Welcome to Big Bear. What can I sell you folks today?"

"Actually," Joe said, "we don't want to buy anything. We're looking for somebody."

Beth's bright smile remained, but her eyes narrowed as they focused on Joe. "Who might that be?"

"Dr. Nikolai Stavrogin," Joe answered. "He's supposed to have a cabin near here."

"And who wants to know?" Beth responded, dropping the smile completely.

"You'll have to excuse my friend," Gina said quickly. "We've been on the road a long time, and he's a little tired." She shot a look at Joe that told him to shut up. "Dr. Stavrogin is my—uncle. Maybe he's mentioned me when he's been in the store. My name is Gina. We're very close. I think I recall your name from one of his letters."

The smile slowly returned to the gray-haired woman's face. "You're related to that old Russian bear? You should have said so in the first place. When he gets bored, he comes down here and we play chess." Her smile faded again. "Why did you come here looking for him? Is something wrong?"

33

"I hope nothing's wrong," Gina responded. "His assistant at the university called me because he hadn't checked in since he left Washington. That's not like him."

"Now that you mention it," Beth said, "I haven't seen him since he opened his cabin for the summer. He got some supplies and a new fishing rod because his old fly rod got lost on the way up here. He didn't buy enough food to last more than a week, and that was almost two weeks ago. I hope he's okay."

"It's probably nothing," Gina assured her. "But I'd like to go out to the cabin and make sure he's all right."

"Sounds like a good idea," Beth said. "This can be pretty wild country." She wrote the directions to the cabin on a piece of paper and handed it to Gina. "I hope nothing has happened to Nikolai. I'm fond of him."

Gina smiled. "I know."

Joe kept his mouth shut until they were back on the road. "That was pretty slick," he said to Gina. "How did you know that she and Stavrogin were friends?"

Gina shrugged. "Call it woman's intuition. Something in her eyes and her tone of voice. I don't know. It seemed pretty obvious to me."

The map that Beth Truman had drawn led them to a dirt road that meandered up and down hills for a few miles and eventually to a gurgling stream with a rickety plank bridge. Frank, who had taken over the driving, stopped the motor home, got out, and inspected the structure.

"I don't think that bridge and this vehicle were meant for each other," he announced and climbed back into the driver's seat. He pulled the motor home off on the shoulder, parked, and hopped out again.

"Where are you going?" Joe asked.

Frank pointed to a log cabin on a small rise on the far side of the stream. "If the map is right, that's Stavrogin's cabin."

Joe and Gina climbed out and followed Frank across the bridge. "It looks as if somebody's home," Joe noted as they got closer. "There's a car."

Frank didn't wait for the others to catch up. As soon as he reached the cabin, he climbed the steps to the porch and knocked on the front door. "Hello?" he called out. "Dr. Stavrogin? Hello?"

He stopped knocking when Joe and Gina joined him. "I don't think anybody's inside," he said.

"Either that or he's very antisocial," Joe offered.

"There's only one way to find out," Frank

replied, grabbing the doorknob. It turned and the door swung open. Frank poked his head inside. "Hello?" he shouted one more time.

Nobody answered.

Joe edged past his brother and went inside. "I don't think the professor ever took a housekeeping course," he observed as he moved around the single room. Books and clothes were strewn everywhere. A half-eaten sandwich poked out of a pile of papers littering the cabin's only table. A long, thin line of ants marched up and down a table leg, carting off tiny prizes from the forgotten meal.

Frank walked over to the table, brushed away some of the scurrying ants, and touched the bread. It was rock hard. "This is beyond stale," he said. "This is fossilized. Nobody's been here for days, maybe even a week or more."

"If that's Stavrogin's car outside," Joe responded, "where did he go?"

"If the Assassins nabbed him, they wouldn't need his car," Frank noted.

"What would the Assassins want from Dr. Stavrogin?" Gina asked.

"That's what we came to Alaska to find out," Frank answered. He glanced at his watch. "It's getting late. Let's go back to the motor home, get some sleep, and start again in the morning.

Joe squinted at the sunlight streaming in the window. "What are you talking about? It's not even dark yet."

Frank chuckled. 'It's the middle of summer, and we're almost standing on the Arctic Circle."

Joe frowned. "So what?"

"So the sun is up for over twenty hours a day," Frank explained. "And I know from a lifetime of experience that you don't function well on four hours of sleep."

At midnight Joe was seated on one of the parked dirt bikes, watching the sun set while Frank and Gina were sound asleep in the motor home. They had agreed to take turns keeping an eye on the cabin in case somebody showed up. Since the night was more like twilight, Joe didn't have any trouble observing the cabin from across the stream. He did, however, have a lot of trouble staying awake.

Joe had started to nod off for the third or fourth time when he thought he caught a flicker of movement outside the cabin. His head snapped up, and his eyes popped open. He watched and waited. The cabin was dark and silent. Nothing moved anywhere near it, but Joe decided to check it out since he didn't have anything better to do.

He slithered across the bridge on his belly and then hugged the trees that lined the shoulder on the far side. If anybody was in the cabin, Joe wanted to check out the person before he or she spotted him.

About fifty feet from the cabin, Joe saw something that made him stop and flatten himself behind the nearest tree. The front door was wide open. He was sure he had shut it tight when they left. Maybe the wind blew it open, he told himself.

Joe crept closer. He heard a faint rustling sound from inside the cabin, and then saw a man slipping silently out the door. There was enough light for Joe to get a fairly good look at his face—and although Joe had never seen Dr. Stavrogin, he knew this guy wasn't the professor.

Joe was staring at the curly-haired cab driver he'd had to rescue!

The man headed into the woods behind the cabin, and Joe followed. As he moved he heard a twig snap behind him and froze in his tracks, listening. All he could hear now was his own heart pounding. Part of him hoped he'd just imagined the noise. Another part realized he had just walked into a trap.

Joe knew he couldn't just stay there like

a sitting duck. As he whirled around to confront whoever was behind him, a sharp pain exploded at the base of his neck. His vision blurred and dimmed. Joe Hardy slumped to his knees and fell facedown on the ground.

Chapter

5

WHEN JOE opened his eyes, there was a dull ache in his head, and Frank was staring down at him. "What's the matter?" Joe mumbled. "What are you staring at? Did I go bald during the night or something?"

The worry lines on his brother's face faded, and a faint smile appeared on his lips. "Well, I guess you didn't suffer permanent brain damage—no more than usual, anyway."

With a little help from Frank, Joe sat up. "What are we doing in Stavrogin's cabin?" he asked in a bewildered tone as he took in his surroundings.

"I was hoping you could tell me," Frank replied. "I came over here looking for you."

Joe struggled to push through the fog in his brain. "I remember now. . . . I saw somebody in the cabin—the cabdriver who gave us the underwater tour of the Potomac."

"You saw him *here?*" Frank responded.

Joe nodded and instantly regretted it. "I was going to tail him," he said as he rubbed his sore neck, "but somebody else sneaked up behind me and decked me."

"Did you get a glance at the person who knocked you out?"

Joe shook his head and winced. He was going to have to remember not to move his head for a while. "It happened too fast." He paused and frowned. "And it didn't happen in here. I was outside, near the trees."

Frank studied the bruise on the back of Joe's neck. "Whoever hit you was a real pro. He knew how to take you out quickly without killing or maiming you in the process. You're lucky."

"Remind me to thank the Assassin if we ever catch him," Joe grumbled.

"I don't think you were attacked by an Assassin," Frank said.

"You think the cabdriver is an Assassin, but you don't think I was knocked out by an Assassin."

Frank nodded.

"Okay, Joe said with a sigh. "Why not?"

"Think about it," Frank said. "Would an Assassin leave you alive?"

"I hadn't thought of that," Joe admitted. "So who was it?"

"I don't know," Frank replied. "But I could make a pretty good guess."

Joe knew what his brother was thinking. "A Network agent?"

"I hope so," Frank said. "Because if it wasn't, that means a third player is involved, and this case is already complicated enough." He looked around the cluttered room. "Do you know what I think?"

"No," Joe answered, "but I'll bet you're going to tell me."

"I think this mess was made by somebody searching for something."

"Something related to the fishing rod case?" Joe suggested.

"Maybe," Frank said. "The only problem with that theory is that the Assassins already have the case. What else could they be after?"

Joe picked up a nearby pile of papers and started to sift through them. "Let's see what we can find that the Assassins couldn't."

"Good idea," Frank responded, grabbing a book off the floor. He scanned the cover and handed the book to his brother. "Check this out," he said.

Joe read the title out loud: *"Principles of Fusion Energy."* Then he saw the author's name. "Hey! Dr. Stavrogin wrote this."

Frank grabbed another handful of books and scanned the covers. "Here's another one," he announced. *"Dynamics of Fusion Reactions."*

"So Stavrogin's a fusion expert," Joe said. "You don't think the Assassins are trying to corner the fusion energy market, do you?"

"That depends on the kind of fusion energy," Frank replied ominously.

Joe studied his brother carefully. "What do you mean?"

"I mean fusion can do a lot more than crank out electricity for your toaster oven," Frank told him. "An uncontrolled fusion reaction is what makes a hydrogen bomb."

Joe's eyes widened. "We can't let the Assassins get their hands on a hydrogen bomb!"

"If that's what they're after, I don't know if we can do anything about it," Frank said grimly. "It may already be too late."

Their search of the cabin didn't turn up anything that might lead them to Stavrogin or the Assassins, and they finally gave it up when

Gina came looking for them. The Hardys filled her in.

"We can't quit now," Joe insisted as they walked back across the rickety bridge.

Frank stopped and gazed down at the stream. "Nobody said anything about quitting. We just have to figure out what our next move will be."

"I'm not sure I understand all this," Gina said. "Even if Dr. Stavrogin could make a bomb for the Assassins, wouldn't they need uranium or plutonium or something like that?"

"That's right," Joe chimed in. "And that stuff doesn't exactly grow on trees."

"Just because it's hard to get doesn't mean the Assassins don't have it," Frank pointed out. "We have to assume the worst."

Joe nodded up the road toward a cloud of dust. "It looks as if we may have company in a few minutes. A car's coming this way."

"Let's get back to the motor home," Frank said.

"It's just a car," Gina responded. "What's the big deal?"

"Have you seen any other cars on this road?" Frank snapped, grabbing her arm and moving her quickly across the bridge.

"Frank hates coincidences," Joe explained, trotting to keep up with his brother.

"I don't believe in taking unnecessary risks," Frank said, his attention on the approaching car. "Our visitors are driving a Jeep with a camouflage paint job. Would you like to hang around and ask them what they're hunting?"

Gina jerked her arm free from Frank's grip and peered at the car speeding down the road. "What are we going to do?" she asked. "We can't outrun them in the motor home, can we?"

"No!" Joe yelled, breaking into a run. "Our only chance is to lose them in the woods."

He didn't head for the trees, though. He sprinted to the motor home, jerked open the door, rushed inside, and bolted back out seconds later.

"Let's go!" he shouted, jumping on one of the dirt bikes and tossing a key to his brother. Joe jammed his key in the ignition slot of the motorcycle and slammed his foot down on the kick starter. The engine roared to life. He motioned to Gina, and she hopped on behind him.

The Jeep was close enough now for Joe to see the grime on the headlights and the two stone-faced men in the front seat. He noticed that Frank was having trouble starting the other dirt bike. His foot pumped up and down

45

on the kick starter, but the engine only sputtered and died, sputtered and died.

"What's wrong?" Joe called out.

"I don't know!" Frank shouted back. He waved his hand in the air, gesturing toward the forest. "Go on! Get out of here! Don't wait for me!"

"No!" Joe bellowed. He gunned the engine, popped the hand clutch, and spun the bike around. The engine screamed as Joe took the bike onto the road and raced toward the oncoming Jeep, aiming the motorcycle right between the headlights. He bared his teeth in his best mad dog snarl and glared at the driver. At the last second Joe swerved away and zoomed past the Jeep.

He hoped the trick worked; he wouldn't get a second chance. He glanced over his shoulder and saw the Jeep skid to a halt.

His eyes shifted back to the road ahead. An accident now could be fatal. "What are they doing?" he shouted to Gina.

"They're turning around and following us!" Gina yelled in his ear. He could barely hear her over the whine of the engine and the rushing of the wind around them.

Joe slowed down and scanned the woods on either side of the road.

"They're catching up!" Gina cried out.

"Good!" Joe responded as he veered off the road onto a rutted trail that disappeared in the trees. "Are they still behind us?" he yelled, his eyes focused on the rough trail, weaving around potholes and boulders. The dirt bike wasn't made for two riders, so Joe had to be careful. If he rode it too hard, they might take a very ugly spill.

"Yes!" Gina told him. "And they're still gaining on us!"

Joe stole a quick look over his shoulder and saw the Jeep's knobby tires rolling easily over the rocks and ruts that had slowed him down. He couldn't play it safe anymore. He was going to have to push the bike to the limit. He crouched low over the handlebars and leaned hard into a sharp turn around a high rock outcropping.

"Look out!" Gina screamed as they came out of the curve.

Joe's head reared back, and he slammed on the brakes when he saw a second mottled green Jeep blocking the trail. Two men wearing matching camouflage jumpsuits stood in front of the Jeep. The submachine guns in their hands told Joe this was the end of the line.

Chapter

6

"GET OFF the bike," one of the men ordered roughly.

Joe decided not to argue. The weapon in the man's hands could cut a person in half with a single squeeze of the trigger.

The man giving the orders wore a baseball cap printed with the same camouflage pattern as his jumpsuit. The other man had close-cropped black hair. In addition to the stubby submachine guns they carried, they also had large hunting knives hanging upside down in sheaths strapped to their jumpsuits, just below their left shoulders.

Joe had seen men dressed this way before: soldiers ready for combat.

Holding the submachine gun in one hand, the guy in the cap unhooked a radio from his waist with his free hand and spoke into it. "This is Delta team. We have them."

The radio crackled and a static-filled voice said, "You know what to do."

Joe held his breath and clutched Gina's hand, hoping the voice on the radio hadn't just issued their death warrants.

"Get in the Jeep," the man said flatly.

Joe breathed again. "You go on ahead," he replied, trying to sound glib. "We'll follow you."

The silent man with the short black hair let out a low chuckle. The other man's lips twitched. "I don't think so," he said. "Just do as you're told, and this will all be over in a few minutes."

"That's what worries me," Joe muttered as he climbed into the backseat.

Gina rode in the front seat next to the driver, the black-haired guy. The man giving the orders sat next to Joe.

"Nice hat," Joe remarked, nodding at the green-and-brown cap the man was wearing. "Where can I get one?"

The man shifted his eyes and glared at Joe. "Do us all a favor and shut up," he said gruffly.

The man's coldness told Joe that he wouldn't

want to find out what would happen if he didn't shut up. So they rode in silence as the Jeep bounced along the trail, moving farther into the Alaskan wilderness. The Jeep that had originally chased Joe and Gina had not followed. Joe hoped it hadn't gone back for Frank.

After a while they rolled to a stop. "End of the line," the man in the cap announced.

"I don't think I like the sound of that," Joe said.

"You don't have to like it," the man said. "You won't be here that long."

"I don't think I like the sound of that, either," Joe responded.

The two armed men marched Joe and Gina single-file into the woods. Joe caught a glimpse of movement ahead, and then another glimpse off to the side. Then he spotted a large green camouflage tent and knew then that they were in the middle of some kind of paramilitary base hidden amid the trees. There were tents, men, and equipment scattered all around. The green and brown splotches and swirls that covered every man-made surface blended in perfectly with the natural surroundings, making the camp virtually invisible from any distance.

The black-haired member of the Delta team ducked into the large tent and came back out a minute later, followed by a nondescript man of average height and unremarkable build.

Despite his completely forgettable looks, the man's face was etched deeply in Joe's memory.

"Mr. Gray," Joe greeted the extraordinarily ordinary man. "I should have known you were behind all this.

"I almost didn't recognize you out of uniform," Joe added. Mr. Gray—the Gray Man— got his name from the bland gray suits he always wore. Joe had no idea what his real name was, and sometimes he suspected the Gray Man had forgotten it himself.

The Gray Man smiled down at his military-style camouflage outfit. "I like to blend into the background wherever I am," he said.

The Gray Man held open the tent flap. "There are some things we should discuss privately."

"Wait a minute,' Joe said. "What about Frank? Is he all right?"

The Gray Man nodded behind Joe. "See for yourself."

Joe glanced back over his shoulder and saw Frank coming toward them, flanked by two armed guards.

"So much for my great diversion," Joe grumbled. "You were supposed to take off

51

into the woods while I led these guys on a wild-goose chase.''

''I did,'' Frank said, ''but the woods were crawling with Network agents.''

''We've been watching you ever since you showed up at Stavrogin's cabin,'' the Gray Man explained as they slipped into the spacious tent. He sat down in a folding chair and gestured to the Hardys and Gina to do the same.

''Why did you have the cabin staked out?'' Frank asked. ''And where is Dr. Stavrogin now?''

''I didn't bring you here to answer your questions,'' the Gray Man said curtly.

''I think you owe us some kind of explanation,'' Frank responded coolly. ''First, one of your men attacks my brother, and then you kidnap us.''

''That's right!'' Joe snapped. ''We may be way out in the middle of nowhere—but we're still in the United States, and there are laws!''

The Gray Man smiled and clapped his hands slowly. ''Very good. Very convincing. Feel free to report this incident to the local authorities.'' He leaned forward, and a cold, hard expression settled on his face. ''But when you do, keep a few points in mind.'' He stuck his index finger up. ''One: You've been on federal land ever since you got within a mile of Stavrogin's cabin. The state and county governments have no authority here." He held up another finger. "Two: Officially, the Network doesn't exist, and neither do I. You can tell the police I kidnapped you, but they won't find anybody to arrest."

He paused and took a deep breath. "Three," he said, jabbing a third finger in the air. "This is a very sensitive national security issue. You could jeopardize the entire operation, putting millions of lives at risk."

"Since nobody will believe us, anyway," Frank said, "couldn't you at least tell us what this is all about?"

The Gray Man shook his head. "I'm sorry. That's out of the question."

"Okay," Frank responded. "Let me tell you what I think is going on. We know Dr. Nikolai Stavrogin is a nuclear physicist involved in fusion research, and fusion is the heart of a thermonuclear explosion. We also know the Assassins are very resourceful. If any terrorist group could build a hydrogen bomb, they'd be at the top of the list."

"I'm still listening," the Gray Man said.

"Hold on," Gina cut in. "What does any of this have to do with the two guys who killed Solomon?"

The Gray Man's gaze shifted to Gina, and he seemed to soften. "I know you've been through a lot. If it's any comfort, I don't think Mr. Mapes was actually involved with the Assassins. He just got caught up in something that was out of his control."

"Stavrogin's fishing rod case is the key, isn't it?" Frank prodded. "What was in it that the Assassins wanted so badly?"

The Gray Man sighed. "I have to hand it to you boys. You certainly are persistent. I never dreamed you'd get this far." He stood up and started to pace the floor. "I guess I'll have to tell you enough to satisfy your curiosity.

"The Russians were working on fusion reactors long before we were," he began, "and Stavrogin was one of their top fusion experts before he came to the U.S. Recently he got involved in some classified fusion research for our government. Without telling anyone, he took some very sensitive notes with him when he came up here to his fishing cabin."

"And he hid the notes in the fishing rod case," Frank ventured.

The Gray Man nodded.

"But the case got sidetracked to Atlanta by the luggage theft ring," Joe added.

"I have no idea what happened to Stavrogin's fishing rod case," the Gray Man responded with a wry chuckle. "We're still looking for it, but I doubt if we'll ever find it. It was probably snatched by somebody who liked the case or wanted a new fishing rod. We planted a fake case. That's the one the Assassins grabbed in Atlanta."

"Hold on," Frank interrupted. "What made you think the Assassins would go to Atlanta to look for it?"

"I assigned two Network agents to protect Stavrogin while he was in Alaska," the Gray Man replied, "and he told them about the notes as soon as he found out the fishing rod was missing. Then we got lucky and spotted two known Assassins boarding a flight from Anchorage to Atlanta, but they gave us the slip in Atlanta. A little digging uncovered the luggage theft problem at Eddings Air, and we put two and two together."

"So you set a trap for the Assassins," Frank said.

"We took some copies of Stavrogin's old notes," the Gray Man continued, "altered them to make the information worthless, and put the papers in the fishing rod case—along with a hidden transmitter. We hoped the two Assassins would bring the case back to Alaska and lead us to their base. But they got rid of the case before they left Atlanta."

"By now the Assassins must know the papers they took from the case are worthless," Joe remarked.

"Of course," the Gray Man responded. "Why do you think they went back to Stavrogin's cabin?"

Frank juggled all these new facts in his mind and realized something was still missing. "You haven't told us everything," he said bluntly. "How did the Assassins know about the fishing rod case in the first place? And where is Dr. Stavrogin now?"

The Gray Man sat down heavily, gazed at the ground for a moment, and cleared his throat. "We think the Assassins bugged Stavrogin's phone in Washington. And when Stavrogin called his assistant and asked for his notes to be sent to him in a fishing rod case, the Assassins knew just what to look for." The Gray Man heaved a deep sigh. "I should have assigned more men to watch Stavrogin. While I was in Atlanta, the Assassins kidnapped him up here in Alaska, and both of the Network agents guarding him were badly injured in the attack. That's why I have a small army here now. Sooner or later the Assassins will pry the information they need out of Stavrogin. We can't let that happen."

"What can we do to help?" Joe asked.

The Gray Man's gaze was as cold as his answer. "Go home and stay there."

The Gray Man refused to answer any more questions and had one of his men drive the Hardys and Gina back to the motor home.

"At least they brought my motorcycle back," Joe noted.

Frank knelt down next to the dirt bike that had refused to start earlier. He twisted a section of rubber tubing that snaked down from the gas tank. "There was a crimp in the fuel line. It should start now."

He got up, grabbed the handlebars, swung his right leg over the seat, and pumped the kick starter with his foot. "Want to race?" Frank challenged his brother.

Joe looked around. "Where?"

Frank shrugged. "We'll figure it out when we get there."

"Are you just going to leave me here?" Gina asked as Joe jumped on the second dirt bike.

"Don't worry," Frank called out as he sped away from the motor home. "We'll be back before dark!"

Joe gave his brother a curious look when he caught up with him. They both knew it was only the middle of the afternoon—and the sun wouldn't set until almost midnight.

* * *

From a clump of bushes on a high hill overlooking a shallow creek, the Hardys stared down at the stand of birch and pine concealing the Network camp.

"This is stupid," Joe muttered. "I can't see anything but trees."

"When they move out, we'll be able to see them," Frank assured him.

"Move out? Where are they going? Did the Gray Man say anything about moving out?"

"It was what he *didn't* say," Frank explained. "The Network agent who knocked you out was part of a surveillance team. They must have followed our buddy the suicidal cabdriver back to the Assassins' secret base. I'm sure the Gray Man is getting ready to raid that base and rescue Dr. Stavrogin. All we have to do is sit and wait."

Joe was about to ask how long they were going to wait when he heard the approaching drone of an engine. A three-wheeled all-terrain vehicle with balloon tires crested the hill and stopped twenty feet from it. Another ATV appeared behind it.

Frank shrank back in the bushes, pulling his brother with him, and peered out through the leaves at the ATVs. Could the Network agents have fooled them again? Frank wondered. If they weren't Network operatives, then—

Frank shuddered. He knew the Assassins wouldn't let them get away alive this time.

Frank held his breath and watched as two grim-faced men got off the ATVs silently, crossed the hillside, and headed straight for where he and his brother were hiding.

Chapter

7

THE TWO MEN stopped a few feet from the Hardys, but their eyes weren't on the bushes; they were peering down the steep hill into the Network camp.

Joe stared at the men. Both had scraggly black hair, badly in need of a trim, and one of them had a full beard, while the other had several days of stubble on his face. Next, Joe's eyes traveled down to the men's weapons. He knew what the fat green tubes were, and he didn't think they were standard issue for federal agents.

Assassins, Joe thought grimly.

A shock ran through him when the large bearded man slid out his telescoping rear blast tube, flipped up the front sight, and rested the yard-long contraption on his shoulder.

The hand-held rocket launcher, powerful enough to rip apart a tank, wasn't pointed at the Hardys. The bearded man had aimed it downhill, right at the heart of the Network base.

Joe didn't wait for the other man to get his weapon ready. "No!" he screamed, charging out of the bushes and lunging at the bearded Assassin.

The man whirled at the sound of Joe's voice, and Joe suddenly found himself staring at the tip of the deadly rocket packed inside the tube. He darted under the weapon, shoving it up and out of the way with one hand while he rammed his head into the Assassin's stomach.

The man made a soft grunt, and the rocket launcher made a thunderous *whoomp!* Searing hot air from the backblast shriveled the grass inches from Joe's face as the big bearded man stumbled backward and the two of them tumbled to the ground. Joe grappled the rocket launcher away from the man and heaved it down the side of the steep hill.

Frank hit the other Assassin with a flying karate kick while the man was still fumbling with the blast tube extension. His opponent was quick, snapping his head and shoulders back and only taking a glancing blow on the chest. The Assassin countered with a round-house kick that slammed into Frank's back, sending him sprawling on the ground.

Joe and Frank both scrambled to their feet as the Assassin jerked out the blast tube, whipped the weapon onto his shoulder, and squeezed the trigger. The Hardys landed on him just as the rocket was unleashed. Joe didn't hear the blast this time. He was still deaf from the last one. But he did see an orange fireball engulf the trees near the creek below.

He didn't know if the rocket had hit the Network camp, and he didn't have much time to think about it. Frank was already on his feet, chasing the bearded man, who was making a dash for the three-wheeled ATVs. The other Assassin quickly rolled away from Joe and jumped up. Joe started to get up—but fell back down and hugged the ground when the Assassin took a swipe at him with the rocket launcher, swinging the empty tube like a base-ball bat.

The man raised the weapon over his head and brought the metal tube whistling down. Joe twisted out of the way and heard the weapon slam into the ground with a dull thud.

Suddenly Joe realized he was at the edge of

the hill, and he could feel himself slipping down the steep slope. The Assassin was glaring down at him, and Joe could see the cold fury in the man's gaze. For a second he was sure the terrorist was going to leap on top of him, sending them both tumbling down the rocky slope and probably breaking both their necks.

Then there was a shout from the top of the hill, and the man spun around and sprinted toward the ATVs, where Frank was grappling with the bearded terrorist.

Digging his heels into the earth and clutching clumps of grass, Joe stopped his slide and clawed back up the hill. Those few short seconds were all the Assassins needed to make their getaway.

When Joe reached Frank, he found his brother on his knees, groaning softly and grasping his side. Joe ran over to his brother and helped him up. "Are you okay?" he asked.

Frank grimaced and nodded. "I didn't see that second guy coming up behind me. He clobbered me with a kidney punch." Shrugging off Joe's gentle but firm grip, he dashed over to the dirt bikes. "Come on!" he shouted. "We can still catch them!"

Frank and Joe jumped on the dirt bikes and took off after the Assassins. The ATVs were already out of sight in the dense woods, but the three wide tires left tracks that were easy to follow. Frank led the way, weaving through the trees, ducking under low-hanging branches, and glancing back frequently to make sure Joe was still with him.

When the tracks dipped down and across a narrow creek bed, Frank gunned the engine, stood up on the foot pegs, tugged hard on the handlebars, and leaned forward as the light-weight motorcycle sailed across the small stream. Joe watched his brother's bike come down in a perfect two-point landing, back wheel first, just as he hit the air himself.

Joe's brief flight ended with a jarring impact on the other side of the creek. His front wheel hit the ground and turned slightly to one side, and the bike wobbled and bucked, almost throwing him off. Joe grappled with the handle-bars and wrestled the bike, refusing to let it crash. The rear tire swerved violently one way and then the other, but Joe stayed with it and brought the bike back under control.

Frank caught a glimpse of one of the ATVs up ahead and pushed the dirt bike even harder. He rode in a crouch, barely touching the seat, his legs and arms taking the jarring shock as the tires bounced over the rocky, bumpy forest floor. He was gaining on the rear

ATV now. He could see the twin back tires churning up the ground and spewing out a spray of dirt and leaves. The rider bobbed his head slightly as he drove between two large pines and then glanced back over his shoulder at Frank.

Frank wondered why the Assassin had ducked, since there was plenty of headroom beneath the lowest branch of either tree. The rider glanced back at him again, and Frank had the sense that the man was waiting for something to happen.

The answer came to Frank in a shaft of sunlight glinting off a shiny, thin strand of wire strung between the two pine trees. His eyes widened, and he heaved himself backward off the bike.

"Trip wire!" he screamed just before he smashed into the ground with a painful thud. The motorcycle rolled under the razor-thin metal strand that would have taken Frank's head off, kept going for another fifteen feet, took a wild hop over a rock, and crashed on its side.

Joe hit the brakes, cut the front wheel sharply to the left, and skidded to a halt. He jumped off the bike and ran over to his brother.

Frank waved him off. "I'm all right! Don't let them get away! I'll catch up!"

Joe didn't argue. He hopped back on the dirt bike and took off on the Assassins' trail. The tire tracks wound through the forest for another mile or so and then headed across a wide clearing.

The ATVs were nowhere in sight—and the tracks led straight to the edge of a jagged cliff that was near Stavrogin's cabin. Joe got off the motorcycle and stood near the edge. Almost a thousand feet below was a vast canopy of green treetops that extended into the distance. The far horizon was rimmed with mountain peaks.

He was still standing there when Frank arrived on his crippled dirt bike. The front wheel was badly bent, and Frank had a hard time controlling the bike if he tried to go faster than ten miles an hour.

"Do you think they rode over the cliff and killed themselves?" Joe asked.

Frank's gaze swept the trees that crowded the base of the cliff. "It's impossible to tell from here. You could hide a small city in those woods. But why would they kill themselves?"

"To avoid being captured?" Joe ventured.

Frank shook his head. "Unlikely. They weren't vastly outnumbered or anything like that. In fact, they probably thought their booby trap sliced me in half. Would two trained Assassins commit suicide if a lone, un-armed teenager was chasing them?"

"Gee, thanks," Joe grumbled. "You make me sound like a first-class weenie."

Frank grinned. "You haven't worked your way up to first class yet."

Before going back to the motor home, the Hardys decided to stop at the Network camp. Even though the Gray Man had made it clear that the Hardys were definitely not welcome within a thousand miles of the Network opera-tion, Frank and Joe wanted to make sure ev-erybody was all right after the rocket attack.

Joe was prepared for the worst. A rocket designed to blast apart thick steel tank armor could do a lot of serious damage. But he wasn't prepared for what they found.

"It's as though the Network camp was never here," Joe said after they had combed the area for any sign of the men and gear that had been there earlier in the day. The only indication that anything other than birds and bears had touched this part of the wilderness was the ring of scorched trees and the smolder-ing crater left by the antitank rocket.

"Of course," Frank muttered. "I should

have thought of this. They wouldn't stay here after the rocket attack. They'd move the camp to a safer location, and hopefully one where the Assassins couldn't find them.''

''And any plans to rescue Dr. Stavrogin would have to be put on hold,'' Joe added.

Frank nodded. Suddenly he felt very tired, and his body ached in a dozen places. ''It's been a long day,'' he said wearily. ''Let's get back to our own base camp, have something to eat, and go to sleep.''

''That sounds like a good plan to me,'' Joe agreed, climbing back on his bike.

They soon discovered they were going to have to wait a little longer than they had anticipated. And any hopes they might have built up about Gina waiting for them with a nice, hot dinner were quickly forgotten, too.

''What happened to the motor home?'' Joe cried out when they reached the rickety bridge over the stream near Stavrogin's cabin. ''It's gone!''

Chapter

8

"THERE'S PROBABLY a perfectly logical explanation for this," Frank said calmly, studying the vacant spot where they had left Gina and the motor home a few hours earlier.

"It may be logical," Joe responded, "but that doesn't mean we're going to like it."

"Let's try to reason this out," Frank said. "Where could Gina have gone?"

Joe sat down in the grass by the roadside. "Maybe she got tired of waiting for us to come back."

"That's a possibility," Frank conceded. "Here's another: Somebody scared her off or forced her to leave."

"The Network?" Joe ventured.

"Or the Assassins," Frank said grimly.

Even though he was bone tired and sore all over, Joe got up and climbed back on the battered dirt bike. "We'd better start looking for her."

Frank squinted at the sun on the horizon and shook his head. "It'll be dark soon. We'll start in the morning."

Frank and Joe spent the night in Stavrogin's deserted cabin. In the morning there was still no sign of Gina or the motor home.

"I'm starving," Joe complained as he helped Frank take off the bent front wheel of the dirt bike. Using some tools they had found in the cabin, they managed to work most of the wobble out of the wheel.

Frank slipped the wheel back onto the fork, tightened the axle nuts, and reconnected the front brake line. "That should hold it until we get to Big Bear," he said.

Joe looked at him. "Why are we going to Big Bear?"

"To get a new wheel and something to eat," Frank replied, swinging his leg over the seat and starting the engine. "And to ask some questions," he added.

An hour later the Hardys found themselves at the counter of the Mooseburger Café. They had just dropped Frank's bike at the gas station for repairs and been told that it would take around a week to get a new wheel. The café was deserted except for a large man in an apron who lumbered over and handed them menus. He had long blond hair tied back in a braid, and Joe counted five gold hoops piercing his left ear.

"What'll it be?" the man asked in a deep, friendly voice, smiling down on the Hardys and flashing several gold teeth.

"Do you really have mooseburgers?" Joe asked. He was pretty sure he didn't want one, but he had to ask.

The big man chuckled. "Nah, that's my name. Simon Mooseburger. I own the joint. I do most of the cooking, too."

Mooseburger took their order and came back a few minutes later with two large plates piled high with food: stacks of buttered toast, mounds of hash brown potatoes, and huge omelets bursting with steaming hot cheese. Joe wolfed his down and then attacked his brother's plate after Frank announced he was stuffed.

"Looks like you saved me the trouble of washing these," Mooseburger remarked as he took away the empty plates that Joe had practically scraped clean. "Can I get you boys anything else?"

"You could answer a couple of questions," Frank said.

Mooseburger cocked his head to one side and raised his eyebrows. "What kind of questions?"

"We're looking for a friend of ours," Frank explained. "She might have passed through town sometime late yesterday." Frank described Gina.

Mooseburger shook his head. "If she came through Big Bear, she didn't stop here. Or if she did, I didn't notice her. Business may be a little slow right now, but it starts to pick up around noon. I see a lot of tourists every day."

"She was driving a big brown motor home," Joe said. "Maybe you noticed that."

The blond man shrugged. "I see a lot of those, too. Motor homes aren't unusual in these parts."

Something in the tone of his reply made Frank ask, "Have you seen anything unusual lately?"

"You might say that," Mooseburger said. "Most of the traffic up here is tourists and gold miners. So I see a lot of station wagons, motor homes, and small pickup trucks.

"I know most of the local prospectors," he

continued. "They're all small-time operators. The big mines were played out a long time ago. So I was sort of surprised when heavy-duty trucks started rolling through town a few months ago. Then a couple of tight-lipped strangers started buying supplies at the general store."

"Tell us more about these strangers," Frank said. "What do you think they're doing up here?"

"I don't think they came for the fishing," Mooseburger replied. "Fishermen like to talk. Prospectors, on the other hand, keep their mouths shut. They think everybody's out to jump their claim. If they strike a gold vein, the last thing they want to do is talk about it."

"So you think these guys were looking for gold?" Frank asked.

Mooseburger shook his head. "I think they *found* gold."

"Really?" Joe responded, intrigued and excited by the idea. "Where?"

"As near as I can figure," Mooseburger said, "they've opened up the old McDonald mine."

Joe snorted. "Oh, sure. I get it. Old McDonald had a mine, right?"

"No, I'm serious," the blond hulk re-

73

sponded, sounding slightly offended. "I'll show you." He disappeared into the kitchen for a minute and came back with a topographical map that showed every hill and valley in the area. "Here," he said, jabbing a finger at the map. "The McDonald mine is right at the base of this cliff."

"Cliff?" Frank echoed, his eyes and ears suddenly doubly alert. A quick study of the map confirmed that the man's finger was resting on a spot not far from Stavrogin's cabin—the cliff from which the two Assassins seemed to have launched themselves into space.

"That's right," Mooseburger said. "It's a big one, too. From the top there's quite a view."

"I know," Frank said. "We've seen it."

The view was just as impressive the second time—and the cliff was just as sheer. "I don't see any way those two Assassins could have gotten down this wall without breaking their necks," Joe remarked. "And even if they could climb down, what did they do with the ATVs?"

"I don't know," Frank said, scanning the sea of green treetops below. "But it has to be more than coincidence that they disappeared at the same cliff where the locals think a bunch of mysterious strangers are working an abandoned gold mine. I think the Assassins are using the mine shaft as a secret base.''

Joe looked over the edge, down to the forest more than nine hundred feet below. "So what do you suppose those two guys did? Fly?''

Frank suddenly dropped to the ground, pulling Joe down with him. "Maybe they did,'' he said in a hushed tone, pointing to the canopy of trees below.

Joe saw a section of the treetops near the base of the cliff flutter, falling away to reveal a small cargo helicopter. "Camouflage netting,'' he whispered. "That chopper's big enough to lift one of those small all-terrain vehicles.''

"Come on,'' Frank said, backing away from the cliff edge and jumping to his feet. "They'll spot us out here in the open.'' He ran over to the dirt bike they had shared and pushed it back under the cover of the trees.

Joe stared down at the helicopter for a few more seconds. When the rotor blades started to turn, quickly picking up speed, Joe scrambled up and followed his brother out of the clearing and into the deep shadows of the forest.

The steady *whup whup whup* of the rotor

blades chopping the air grew steadily louder, and the helicopter burst into view, rising above the cliff and then swinging toward the woods. Joe held his breath, waiting for the chopper to pass—but it didn't. Instead, it hovered overhead, as if it could see right through the thick foliage and knew exactly where the Hardys were.

Joe told himself that was impossible. He told himself the pilot would soon move away, off toward some distant objective.

But the helicopter didn't budge. The tree branches swayed in the stiff wind created by the spinning rotor blades. The deafening roar of the helicopter filled Joe's ears, drowning out all other sound—except for a rapid clatter that punctured the wall of noise in short, sharp bursts.

Joe jumped back in shocked surprise, flattening himself against a tree trunk as the ground around him abruptly erupted in a line of tiny explosions. A splintered tree limb fell to the ground at Joe's feet.

The machine gun in the helicopter chattered away, chewing up the earth all around the Hardys. Frank and Joe glanced at each other. They both knew there was no way out. They were surrounded by a deadly hail of bullets.

Chapter

9

THE SHOOTING stopped as abruptly as it had begun. Joe pushed away from the tree, ready to make a desperate dash through the woods. Frank snagged his wrist and held him tightly.

"They might not know exactly where we are!" Frank shouted over the loud thrum of the helicopter swaying above the trees. "They could be trying to flush us out! If we run, they'll cut us down!"

"We know exactly where you are!" a sharp voice boomed from a megaphone overhead. "Do not attempt to escape! Walk out slowly into the clearing with your hands on your heads!"

Joe checked with Frank, who shook his head.

Another burst of machine-gun fire whizzed through the branches. One bullet hit the front tire of the dirt bike. Another one plowed into the rear tire a split second later. A third round punctured the fuel tank, and all the gas quickly drained out of the ragged hole.

"Move now!" the amplified voice barked. "We have the girl." The unspoken threat was clear. If the Hardys didn't follow orders, Gina would be killed.

"We got her into this," Joe said grimly. "We have to do whatever we can to get her out." He turned and trudged toward the clearing.

Frank didn't argue. He knew Joe was right. Besides, they weren't dead yet. As long as they were alive, they had a chance to get out of this mess. Raising his hands over his head, he followed his brother out of the woods.

The helicopter settled down in the clearing, and the big bearded Assassin who had attacked the Network camp got out. This time, instead of a rocket launcher, he was holding a large, belt-fed machine gun in both hands. Frank knew a single slug from that monster could make a hole big enough to throw a football through.

The Assassin had a sinister grin on his face as he jabbed the Hardys with the barrel of his weapon and herded them into the cargo bay. He and the pilot of the helicopter had a rapid exchange of words in a language Frank didn't understand, and the bearded man's fierce smile faded away. He glowered at the Hardys and slammed the sliding door shut.

"My friend doesn't think we need both of you," the pilot shouted over the noise of the engine and the whirling rotors as the helicopter lifted into the air. Frank couldn't detect any accent in his English.

"Boris would like to throw one of you out of the helicopter to see if you can fly," the pilot continued with a chuckle. "I told him the flying lessons would have to wait. Boris has very little patience and a great deal of anger—not very good traits for a man in our profession."

"Oh, sure," Joe responded bitterly. "It's important to stay cool and detached while you're murdering people."

"Quite so," the pilot said. The helicopter dropped rapidly. Trees rose up and shot past on both sides. Joe was sure one of the rotor blades would smack into a nearby tree, snap off, and send the chopper spinning out of control to a fiery crash. Instead, the landing was so smooth, Joe wasn't even sure they *had* landed.

"You must have cool nerves and steady hands to be an Assassin," the pilot said in a tone so casual it sent a chill down Frank's spine.

The pilot led the Hardys out of the helicopter, and the man he called Boris hauled the camouflage netting over it.

Joe didn't even see the entrance to the mine—the old McDonald mine, he presumed—until they were right in front of it. Decades of brush had grown up around the opening, and the Assassins had been careful to maintain its covering.

Inside it was all transformed. The old rafters had been shored up with new timbers, and electric lights, strung along the ceiling of the low, narrow tunnel, glared harshly against the bare rock. A distant hum told Joe there was a generator someplace, cranking out power for the lights.

The Hardys followed the pilot through the tunnel. At a fork in the underground maze the pilot led them off to the right.

"I don't think we've been properly introduced," Joe said to the pilot as they walked. "I'm Joe Hardy, and this is my brother, Frank. What's your name?"

"You can call me Bob," the pilot answered.

"Uh-huh," Joe responded. "Bob the Assassin. I like it. It's kind of catchy."

The pilot chuckled as he stopped in front of a door embedded in the stone wall. "You have a sense of humor," he noted, sliding back a steel bolt to unlock the door. "An admirable trait for one in your situation."

"What situation is that?" Frank asked as the pilot ushered them through the doorway.

"A situation that could easily lead to your untimely death," the pilot said nonchalantly. He stood in the doorway for a moment, gave the Hardys his bone-chilling smile, and then slammed the door on them.

Frank heard the bolt slide home, and then the echo of the pilot's footsteps fading away as he went back down the tunnel. He turned to check out their surroundings. They were locked in a small room carved out of solid rock. A single folding cot in one corner was the only furniture. A dim light bulb hung from the ceiling and bathed the room in a sickly yellow glow.

"That's the last time I let you make the reservations," Joe declared. "I've heard of no-frills hotels, but this is ridiculous."

The room suddenly went dark. Joe heard something smash on the floor, followed by a crunching noise.

"Okay, I think it's safe to talk now," Frank said. "I ripped out the fixture. If there was a mike in there, what's left of it is now on the bottom of my shoe."

"Terrific," Joe muttered. "It wasn't gloomy enough in here before. This new lighting scheme really cheers me up. I've seen brighter tombs."

The door burst open then, and light from the tunnel flooded into the room. A large shadow fell across the floor, obscuring the shattered remains of the light fixture.

"Boris! How are you?" Joe greeted the scowling, bearded man.

The Assassin waved the Hardys out of the small room with a stubby black submachine gun and marched them back to the main tunnel, then down the other branch of the fork. The shaft slowly twisted downward. They passed several more featureless doors. Frank noticed that they were all made of new, unpainted lumber, which meant they were a recent addition. The Assassins had apparently spent time modifying the old mine for their secret purposes.

"Halt!" Boris barked as they came to the fourth door. He pushed Frank aside and knocked on the door. It was a light, polite knock, not the fierce pounding Frank would expect from the angry Assassin. Somebody important was on the other side, somebody Boris feared.

The door swung open, and the pilot—Bob—stood there, regarding the Hardys impassively. "I had hoped to learn more about you—indirectly—before having this little chat. Unfortunately, you made that impossible."

"Looks as if you were right about that bug," Joe said to his brother. "It *was* in the light fixture."

Bob stepped aside to let them into the room, where Gina was sitting on the edge of a folding chair.

"I tried to tell them we could deliver the plans," she said, her tone brash. Joe could see an urgency in her gaze.

"Ah, of course we can," he responded with absolutely no idea what they were talking about.

"I told them how we all stole luggage," Gina said rapidly, the words rushing out in a torrent. "I told them how we found Stavrogin's plans in the fishing rod case and took them because we thought we could sell them back to him or the highest bidder.

"That's right," Frank said, catching on. "Stavrogin's real notes are in a safe place. If you kill us, you'll never find them."

"Your story is interesting," Bob responded. "I'm not saying I believe it, but it is interesting." He paused for a moment and then called out in the foreign tongue that Frank couldn't identify. It might have been Hungarian or Russian or any of a dozen other languages.

Boris stomped into the room and listened while Bob issued terse, mysterious commands. The bearded Assassin nodded, then abruptly grabbed Joe with one beefy hand and dragged him out of the room.

"Hey!" Frank heard his brother cry out from the passageway. "Get your hands off me! I can walk fine by myself!"

The Assassin who called himself Bob smiled almost imperceptibly at Frank and Gina. "I'm afraid I cannot offer you any money for Dr. Stavrogin's papers. I can only offer you your friend's life."

Chapter

10

TWO ASSASSINS and Bob marched Frank and Gina back to the helicopter. One of them was the man who had been with Boris during the rocket attack on the Network camp. Frank hadn't seen the other one before. That meant there were at least five terrorists using the old mine as a base: Bob, Boris, the cabdriver, and these two. Frank wished he could find out if there were more. Knowing the exact number of the enemy could make the difference between life and death for Joe.

The helicopter might be able to carry six or seven at the most, Frank guessed, and Bob appeared to be the only pilot, as well as the leader of the group. Assuming they would use the chopper for a quick getaway, Frank hoped that meant there weren't more than six Assassins stationed in the mine.

Bob flew them to the motor home, which had been driven to a campsite at the end of a dirt road several miles from Stavrogin's cabin.

"This is as far as I got when I ran for it," Gina told Frank.

"You have six hours to deliver Stavrogin's notes," the pilot called out as Frank and Gina climbed out of the helicopter.

"Six hours?" Frank reacted in dismay. "That's not enough time!"

The Assassin shrugged. "It's all the time your friend has."

Frank started to protest, but the chopper was already lifting off, swinging around as it rose in the air. A few seconds later it was whisking back the way it had come.

Frank turned to Gina. "We have to find the Gray Man right away. He's the only one who can help us rescue Joe."

"Yes," Gina agreed. "If Stavrogin was working on a government project, the Network might have copies of his notes. If we could get the copies from the Gray Man, the Assassins would let Joe go."

Frank stared at her. "That's not what I meant."

"But that's the only way to save Joe," Gina said.

"There has to be another way," Frank insisted. "There's no telling what the Assassins might do with the information in Stavrogin's papers."

"What other choice do we have?" Gina responded. "I'm sure the Gray Man would like to send in his crack team of commandos—but at the first sign of a Network agent, Bob, or whatever his name is, will kill Joe." She shivered. "Behind that smiling mask is a cold-blooded killing machine."

"There's no point in arguing now," Frank said, reaching for the door to the motor home. "The first thing we have to do is find the Gray Man."

Frank stepped inside and froze. Someone was there waiting for them, sitting comfortably in a swivel chair.

"Come in and have a seat," the Gray Man said mildly. "We have a lot to talk about."

After Boris had thrown him back in the dark, dungeonlike room, Joe stumbled over to the cot and sat down heavily on it. No doubt about it, this was not one of his better days.

He had no idea what the Assassins had done with Frank and Gina, and it was just starting to sink in that maybe they were in over their heads this time.

He shook his head and told himself to concentrate on his current problem: How was he going to escape? He touched the wall behind him. It was cold, damp, rough, and carved out of solid rock. There was no escape through that.

Then his eyes were attracted by thin streaks of light that seeped in around the door frame. The door was the only way out. He remembered it had a simple lock. Joe figured the room had probably been a storeroom, and the Assassins hadn't planned on running a prison, so they wouldn't have installed a fancy lock.

That was fine with Joe.

He moved over to the door, knelt down, and unlaced one of his high-top sneakers. Running his eye along the left edge of the door, he located the spot where the bolt crossed the narrow gap between the door and the frame. Digging in his pocket, he found a dime, which he carefully tied onto one end of the shoelace. He removed the gum in his mouth and applied a tiny bit to the dime to hold the shoelace in place. Holding the other end above the level of the bolt, he swung the shoelace slowly back and forth, making sure the dime slipped into the gap just below the bolt on each swing. He swung a little harder each time, the weight of the dime acting as a pendulum.

When Joe had the momentum and the timing just right, he gave the shoelace a sharp snap. The dime zipped through the crack, whipped up and around the bolt, and then sailed back through the gap and into Joe's free hand, bringing the other end of the shoelace with it.

Joe tugged the shoelace tightly over the bolt and then slowly pulled back on the top half of the lace without allowing any slack in the lace. He felt the bolt slip out of the notch.

He took a deep breath and tugged the line to the right. The bolt moved a fraction of an inch. He tugged again. The bolt moved a little more. Carefully he worked the bolt back until it cleared the lock plate on the door frame. Joe pushed the door open an inch and peered out into the tunnel. He couldn't see anyone in either direction. So far, so good. He stepped out of the room and started moving cautiously up the passageway.

When he reached the fork in the tunnel, he heard footsteps and low voices coming from the direction of the mine entrance. He had to get out of sight quickly. There was a door a short way down the other branch. He padded over to it, slid back the bolt, and opened the door just wide enough to slip inside. He pulled the door shut and held the handle tightly, hoping no one would notice or care that the door was unlocked.

"What do you want now?" a weary voice with a heavy Russian accent called out from behind him.

Joe spun around to see a tall, bony man hunched over a table littered with papers. He had a long face topped with a cloud of wavy white hair, and there were deep wrinkles at the corners of his eyes.

He leaned forward and studied Joe. "You are not one of them," he stated flatly.

"I'm not?" Joe responded, not sure if that was good or bad. This guy sure didn't look like a terrorist. The tan vest and rust red corduroy shirt he was wearing made him look more like a retired teacher on a fishing trip. Then Joe realized who he was. "Dr. Stavrogin?" he ventured in a hushed voice.

The white-haired man nodded. "And you are?"

Joe held a finger up to his lips and cocked his ear to the door. He didn't hear anything outside and decided he was safe for the moment.

"I'm Joe Hardy," he said as he walked over to the table. He glanced at the array of papers covered with equations, Greek letters, and symbols—none of which he could understand. He looked up at the physicist. "Would you mind telling me what this is all about?"

Stavrogin smiled weakly. "It's a long story."

"That's okay," Joe replied. "I've got plenty of time—I hope."

"Almost anybody can make a low-yield fission device," the Gray Man was telling Frank and Gina.

"You mean an atomic bomb," Frank said.

The Gray Man nodded. "The hardest part is getting enough enriched uranium or plutonium to do the job. A hydrogen bomb, on the other hand, is a lot more complicated."

"And a lot more powerful," Frank added.

"That's right," the Gray Man agreed. "Luckily, the technology and the resources required to build them have ensured that only a handful of nations have hydrogen bombs—until now."

"Something tells me this is where Dr. Stavrogin enters the picture," Frank remarked.

"Stavrogin was working on a fusion energy project," the Gray Man continued. "The trick is to produce a *controlled* fusion reaction without using more energy to contain the reaction than you get in return."

"You're starting to lose me," Gina cut in. "What does fusion energy have to do with hydrogen bombs?"

"I'm getting to that," the Gray Man said. "Stavrogin accidentally stumbled on a simple method for creating an *uncontrolled* fusion reaction."

"And that's exactly what a hydrogen bomb blast is," Frank explained. "An uncontrolled fusion reaction."

The Gray Man nodded solemnly. "With Stavrogin's equations, the Assassins might be able to make a thermonuclear device of untold destructive power."

"How did the Assassins find out about Stavrogin's discovery?" Frank asked.

"His original research wasn't exactly top secret," the Gray Man answered. "Stavrogin wasn't working on a government weapons project. He was trying to harness fusion energy to generate electric power. We threw a tight security net over the whole project as soon as Stavrogin told us about his findings, but obviously we were too late, and the Assassins learned about Stavrogin's work."

"We have to stop them," Frank said.

"We intend to do just that," the Gray Man responded in a cold, distant voice.

Frank's eyes locked on the perfectly ordinary man. "Wait a minute. What are you going to do?"

The Gray Man sighed and stood up. "I had hoped to find a way to penetrate the Assassins' hideout and get Stavrogin out unharmed. But time is running out. As soon as the terrorists find out what they want to know, they'll vanish.

"I came here to convince you to get far away from here before the fireworks start. I've decided to launch a full-scale raid on the mine."

The words hit Frank like hammer blows. "You can't do that," he insisted, clutching the Gray Man's arm. "The Assassins will kill Joe before your men get anywhere near the mine shaft!"

The Gray Man's response was grim. "I'm sorry, Frank, but we'll have to take that risk."

Chapter

11

"THE RAID WILL start just after dark to-night," the Gray Man told Frank and Gina.

Frank glanced at his watch. "Then I still have a few hours to get Joe out myself."

The Gray man shook his head. "I'm sorry. We can't risk your accidentally tipping off the Assassins. That's why I'm leaving two men here to guard you." He pulled a compact radio phone from his coat pocket and spoke into it. "Okay, Thompson, send the men in."

Frank jerked his head toward the window and saw two figures move out of the woods. He made a break for the door, but the Gray Man snared his arm in a tight grip. Frank couldn't shake free. The average-looking man was a lot stronger than average.

While they were struggling, Gina suddenly jumped up and darted toward the door.

"No!" the Gray Man yelled, letting go of Frank and lunging after her.

Gina burst out of the motor home door, smashing it into an unsuspecting Network agent who was about to enter. The agent went sprawling, and Gina rushed past before the other man had time to react.

"Stop her!" the Gray Man yelled.

The second agent whirled around and sprinted after Gina into the woods.

Frank shoved the Gray Man out of the way and jumped out the door. The agent on the ground scrambled up and swung the barrel of his submachine gun at Frank. "Freeze!" he shouted.

Frank hesitated. Three more Network agents rushed out of the forest. He was surrounded.

A short burst of gunfire rang out from the distance. "Cease firing!" the Gray Man barked into the phone. "Cease firing! Who gave the order to shoot?" He turned to the man holding the gun on Frank. "Get him inside," he snapped.

The Network agent nodded at the door. "You heard the man. Move it." Reluctantly

Frank stepped back into the motor home. The agent followed him inside and kept his eyes on Frank all the time.

The Gray Man joined them a few minutes later.

"What happened?" Frank asked. "Where's Gina?"

"She got away," the Gray Man replied.

"What about the gunshots?"

"Just a little accident. One of my men tripped on a rock. He went down, and his weapon went off. Nobody was hit."

"How do you know that one of the bullets didn't hit Gina?" Frank countered.

"If she were lying out there somewhere with a bullet wound," the Gray Man said coolly, "we would have found her.

"I hope she doesn't go back to the Assassins' hideout," he added. "The best we can hope for now is that she'll get lost and be unable to do anything we'll all be sorry for later."

Joe was a little lost himself. Dr. Stavrogin had explained the basic connection between his research and hydrogen bombs, and now the physicist was launching into a full-blown lecture on fusion theory.

"Excuse me," Joe cut in. "This is really

fascinating, and I'd love to hear more about it sometime when we aren't stuck in an old mine shaft crawling with deranged terrorists. Right now, though, I have two important questions."

"I'm sorry," the physicist said. "Sometimes I get carried away. What is it you want to know?"

Joe glanced at the papers on the table. "First, how much information have you given the Assassins already?"

"Very little of any practical use," Stavrogin replied. "Most of these equations are nothing more than what you could find in an advanced textbook. The rest are very intricate false leads."

"Can you produce the right equations without your notes?" Joe asked.

"Oh, yes," the physicist said. "The notes are just helpful reminders." He tapped the side of his head with his finger. "All the critical data are stored in here."

"Then we'd better get moving," Joe said. "And that leads to my second question."

"You have already asked two questions," Stavrogin pointed out.

"I forgot to tell you the first one was a two-parter," Joe responded. "The second question is the really important one. Do you have any idea how we can get out of here?''

Before the physicist could answer, the door burst open and Boris barged into the room. Joe spun around just in time to have a massive fist smashed into his face. The blow hurled him back against the table, which collapsed, and papers flew everywhere. The bearded Assassin thrust the barrel of his submachine gun in Joe's face.

"You've made Boris very angry," a cool voice intoned. The pilot was standing in the doorway. He addressed Boris, and a few sharp words followed in the strange language Joe had heard before. Boris roughly hauled Joe to his feet with his free hand.

"Hi, Bob," Joe said to the pilot as he rubbed his chin. "I got bored in my room, so I decided to take a walk to see what you guys do for fun around here."

The Assassin smiled without his lips parting. "We have a strict rule not to bother the doctor while he's working."

"I'll try to keep that in mind," Joe replied.

"I'm afraid you won't be around long enough to learn the rules," Bob said. "I told your friends you had only six hours to live—but that was before you made a nuisance of yourself. I think it's best to kill you now and deal with the others after they deliver the doctor's notes."

"I don't suppose you'd consider a second opinion," Joe responded.

The Assassin chuckled. "You'd have to convince Boris. He feels responsible for your escape. You made him look bad. So now he must kill you."

Muffled shouts echoed down the tunnel. Bob muttered something to Boris and then abruptly left the room.

Bob wasn't gone long. When he came back, the cabdriver was with him. The curly-haired Assassin hastily scooped up Stavrogin's scattered papers and stuffed them in a backpack.

"There's been a change of plans," Bob announced.

Joe figured that could only be good news for him. Anything that didn't involve a fatal dose of lead poisoning was a definite step up at this point.

The pilot snapped a few orders in the strange language. Boris clearly didn't like what he heard. Joe's hopes grew. If the bearded Assassin was upset by the turn of events, there was a good chance that Joe's execution wasn't on the new agenda—yet.

The Assassins hustled Joe and Dr. Stavrogin out of the mine and into the helicopter.

Three of the terrorists piled into the cargo bay with them while Bob climbed into the pilot's seat and cranked up the huge engine. Boris lingered outside long enough to lob something into the mouth of the mine shaft. Then he sprinted up to the helicopter and jumped in as the ungainly bird started to lift off.

As the chopper cleared the treetops and swung away from the mine, Joe heard a muted *wump* over the loud drone of the whirling rotor blades. Twisting his head to look back out the small window, he saw smoke and dust billow up from where the mine entrance had been.

Joe leaned forward and spoke to the pilot. "I hate to be the one to break the news, but your house just blew up."

The pilot patted the copilot's seat next to him. "Come, sit here," he said gravely. Joe was surprised by the man's serious tone. This was, after all, the same guy who had talked casually about hurling people out of helicopters just to see if they could fly.

Joe climbed into the copilot's seat. The view out the wide, curved windshield was breathtaking—but not because of its beauty. Joe gasped as the green canopy of trees whisked by, only a few feet below the blunt nose of the metal bird.

"You are probably wondering why you're still alive," Bob said.

"The thought crossed my mind," Joe replied, "but I'm not complaining."

"Your life was spared because one of your friends warned us that Network agents were about to attack our camp. Her noble act saved all of us."

"*Her* act?" Joe responded, his full attention now on the pilot. "You mean Gina?"

The Assassin nodded.

"How did she warn you?" Joe asked warily. "Where is she now?"

The pilot's answer came in slow, measured words. "You should be very proud of her. She died with great courage."

"*Died?*" Joe blurted out, unable to contain his shock. "You killed her?"

"She did not die at the hands of an Assassin," Bob said firmly. "She was shot by a Network agent when she escaped from them. She used all her strength and her last breath to warn us about the Network raid. There was nothing we could do for her. The wound was mortal."

Joe heard the words, but it took a while for the meaning to sink in. He put his head in his hands and stared at the hard metal floor of the helicopter.

"Your friend died to save your life," Bob said, putting words to the thoughts spinning in Joe's head. "You owe her a great debt."

"One I can never repay," Joe said harshly.

The Assassin's cold amber eyes studied Joe briefly. "You cannot bring her back to life, but you can punish those who murdered her."

Joe stared at the pilot. "What are you talking about?"

"Join us," Bob replied ardently. "Join the brotherhood of the elite. Become an Assassin."

Frank spent half the brief night pacing the floor of the motor home, waiting for the Gray Man to come back from the raid on the Assassins' hideout, waiting to find out if Joe and Gina were all right.

A Network agent stood by the door, keeping a watchful eye on Frank. Another one was outside, patrolling the area around the motor home.

It was still dark and very late when the Gray Man finally returned. One glance at his haggard, troubled face and Frank knew the news wasn't good.

"What happened?" Frank asked, struggling

to stay calm. "Where's Joe?" He wasn't sure he wanted to hear the answer, but he had to know.

"The Assassins knew we were coming," the Gray Man told him. "They abandoned their base and destroyed everything they couldn't take with them."

"Where's Joe?" Frank repeated tensely.

"I don't know," the Gray Man replied wearily. "I have a team sifting through the rubble. We hope they don't find him."

"They wouldn't kill Joe if they thought there was a chance I'd deliver Stavrogin's notes," Frank insisted, desperately trying to convince himself.

The Gray Man didn't respond, and Frank knew why. They both understood that the Assassins were professional terrorists, cold-blooded killers. The odds were stacked against Joe.

Before Frank could think of anything more to say, he heard a soft tapping at the door. Could it be someone bringing news about Joe? Frank held his breath and focused on the Network guard who opened the door. All at once the guard cried out as a gloved hand grabbed him by the throat and dragged him out into the night.

Before Frank or the Gray Man could react,

a masked figure bounded into the motor home. The intruder was dressed in black from head to foot. Frank couldn't help noticing that even the large automatic pistol in his hand was a flat, dead black. Had the Assassins come to finish them off?

Chapter

12

FRANK FLINCHED as the masked intruder raised the pistol—and tossed it in the air. It landed on the couch with a soft thud, and Frank could see an empty slot in the bottom of the hand grip, where the bullet clip should have been.

"Bang, you're dead," the black-clad figure growled, waving the clip in the air.

Frank would have recognized that voice anywhere. A huge smile of relief spread across his face as the intruder tugged off the black ski mask. The smile quickly faded when he saw the grim determination on Joe's face.

Joe stormed over to the Gray Man, grabbed the front of his jacket with both hands, and glared at the Network director. "You're no better than the Assassins," Joe said bitterly. "You'd kill anybody who got in your way, wouldn't you?"

The Gray Man seemed unfazed by Joe's charge. "This isn't some harmless kid's game. It's a deadly and dangerous business."

"A *business?*" Joe spat out the words. "Get out your calculator and tell me how much a person's life is worth."

"I warned you boys to stay out of this affair," the Gray Man said, pulling away from Joe. "I told you to go home and forget about it. Did you really expect me to blow the whole mission to rescue you from a deep hole after you practically jumped into it?"

"I'm not talking about me," Joe shot back. "I'm talking about Gina!"

"What about Gina?" Frank cut in.

Joe jabbed an accusing finger at the Network director. "He, or one of his men, killed her. It doesn't make any difference. Either way, he's responsible."

Frank put a hand on his brother's shoulder. "Hold on a second. Did you see this happen?"

"No," Joe admitted. He told his brother about the hasty exit from the Assassins' hideout and repeated Bob's version of what had happened to Gina.

"So you didn't even see Gina's body," Frank noted after Joe finished.

"No," Joe replied. "But she's not here, is she? Do you think she's still wandering around in the woods?"

"I think we have to accept the possibility that at least part of the Assassins' story is true," the Gray Man said somberly. "Somehow, they knew about the raid. So Gina probably did make it back to the mine to warn them, hoping that would save Joe."

"What about the rest of the story?" Joe responded sharply.

"You have to admit that it's a little far-fetched," Frank said calmly. "Gina got all the way from here to the mine with a fatal bullet wound?"

"It's more likely that one of the terrorists shot her when she stumbled into the hideout," the Gray Man remarked.

"I didn't hear any shots," Joe argued.

"If you were deep inside the mine," Frank reminded him, "it's possible that you wouldn't have heard a gunshot from near the entrance."

"It's also possible that the Assassins took her outside and shot her after she delivered the warning," the Gray Man added.

Joe stared at him. 'Why would they do that?"

107

"So they could tell you a story about how the Network murdered her," Frank explained, "and recruit you to kill the Gray Man. That's why you're here, isn't it? That's why they let you go?"

Joe's eyes widened with horror at the thought of such a cold, calculated act. But he knew from experience that the Assassins were experts at ruthless cruelty.

He sat down with a sigh that was almost a groan. "You're right," he conceded. "That's just the kind of slimy, ugly thing they would do."

"Let's try to look at the good side," the Gray Man said.

This time Frank and Joe both stared at him in disbelief.

"We have a chance to penetrate the most notorious terrorist group in the world," the Gray Man explained. He looked at Joe. "With you on the inside, we might be able to rescue Dr. Stavrogin and bring the Assassins' whole web of terror crashing down on their heads."

"There's one minor detail," Joe pointed out. "I have to kill you first. Bob called it my initiation rite. Of course, I never planned to carry it out."

The Gray Man shrugged. "If my death is

what it takes, we'll just have to make it happen.''

The sun was rising in the southeast as Frank pushed the last cartridge back into the pistol clip. "All set," he announced, slotting the clip into the housing inside the handgrip. The spring-loaded clip slid home easily in the well-oiled weapon, locking in place with a sharp metallic *snick*.

"We're almost ready here, too," Joe said, taping a small plastic bag to the Gray Man's back. The bag was filled with a sluggish red liquid. "Watered-down catsup makes pretty good blood," he noted. "It's a good thing we have a well-stocked refrigerator."

After he finished taping the bag in place, he checked the string wrapped around the top that held the bag closed. The string was tied in a bow, and one end of the string went up to the Gray Man's shoulder and down his right arm, all the way to his hand. A few thin strips of tape kept the string from slipping.

The Gray Man put his jacket back on slowly and carefully. Another string was hooked by a safety pin to a small rip in a seam in the back of the jacket. That string went down the left sleeve.

"I hope this works," Joe said, picking up the pistol.

Frank scooped up one of the shiny, steel-jacketed lead slugs that were lying on the galley counter. "All you have in that gun are cartridges with detonator caps and enough powder to make a nice loud bang. There's no bullet to hit anything."

Joe turned to the Gray Man. "Remember, when you hear the first shot, pull the left string and then the right."

The Network director smiled. "Don't worry. Even if it doesn't work perfectly, it should be good enough for any prying eyes in the woods. If the Assassins do have a man out there watching, he won't be close enough to see any details. You just have to look like you really want to kill me."

"And you just have to look like you're really dead," Joe replied.

The Gray Man pulled out his radio phone and rattled off a few last-minute orders to the two men outside. "One last thing," he said to the Hardys as he stuffed the compact phone in his jacket pocket. When his hand came out, it wasn't empty. He was holding a small metal disk, about the size of a dime.

"This is a homing device," he explained, handing the disk to Frank. "I always carry it in combat situations in case I get separated from my men and they need to locate me in a hurry.

"You activate it by pressing the point of a sharp object, like a pencil, into a tiny hole on the side. Use it only in an emergency. As long as it's not on, it won't be picked up by any electronic bug detectors the Assassins might have."

Frank took off one of his sneakers, slit open the padded arch support with his Swiss army knife, and wedged the disk inside the padding.

"Good idea," Joe said. "The way your feet smell, that's the last place anybody would want to look."

Frank smiled. "Let's just hope the Assassins are willing to take both of us."

"They already know you're coming with me," Joe replied. "I told them that we were a team."

"Well," Frank said, "I think we've covered everything. Ready?"

The Gray Man moved over to the door and nodded.

Joe took a deep breath. "Let's do it."

"On the count of three," Frank said. "One . . . two . . . three!"

The Gray Man pushed the door open and

jumped out of the motor home. "No! Please!" he screamed. "Don't shoot!"

Joe leapt out after him and swung the pistol into firing position, "You have to pay for Gina!" he shouted at the fleeing man.

Joe squinted down the pistol sight, aiming for the middle of the Gray Man's back. He started to pull the trigger, hesitated, and shifted his aim slightly to the left of his target. He knew Frank had removed all the slugs, but he decided not to take any chances. Finally he squeezed the trigger. The weapon boomed. The spent cartridge flew out. The Gray Man lurched forward and the back of his jacket ripped open. A flow of red seeped out and spread down the jacket.

Joe fired again. His target jerked convincingly, stumbled, and fell facedown.

Frank ran over to the fallen man and knelt beside him. The Gray Man lay still, silent. Frank leaned closer. The dead man opened one eye and gave him a quick wink.

"He's dead!" Frank called out. "You killed him! We'd better get out of here!"

The two Network agents ran around from the far side of the motor home. "Halt!" one of them yelled. "Throw down your weapon!"

Joe bolted for the cover of the trees, with Frank right on his heels. Two submachine guns chattered in unison behind them. None of the bullets flew anywhere near the Hardys, though.

They ran through the woods for over a mile, until they came to a fire road that wasn't much more than an overgrown trail with a pair of parallel ruts outlining it. Joe stopped and pulled a hand-drawn map out of his pocket. He peered up and down the trail.

"This is the spot where Bob said they'd pick us up," Joe said. "I thought they'd be waiting here."

"Maybe they are," Frank responded, pointing up the trail to a solid patch of green that glinted in the early morning sun. "I don't think any metal bushes grow in this climate."

As they walked toward it, the patch of green metal—which was concealed in the tall brush by the side of the road—resolved itself into a stripped-down Jeep with a heavy-duty roll bar and no roof.

"Hello?" Joe called out as they neared the vehicle. "Anybody home?" There was no reply. He waded through the brush to take a closer look.

Frank started to follow, but something about the setup made him nervous. He couldn't shake the feeling that they were walking into a trap, like the wire strung between the two trees that almost took his head off. He had called it a trip wire at the time, but he knew that really wasn't the right term. A trip wire was a trigger that set off a booby trap, and the name came from the fact that it was usually something you tripped over.

Frank froze in his tracks. "Don't move!" he called urgently.

Joe glanced back over his shoulder. "What did you say?" His ankle snagged on something, and he tugged his foot away.

Frank spotted the doubled-over sapling just before it sprung free from the line that held it down. The top half of the tree would whip up, releasing a yard-long sharp stake to fly out straight at Joe's heart.

Chapter

13

FRANK MOVED without thinking. Only his reflexes stood between Joe and a stake whittled down to a needle-sharp point.

The heel of Frank's foot slammed into the back of Joe's knee in a swift side kick. Joe's leg buckled, and he swayed backward. Frank's arms shot out, and he grabbed Joe by the shoulders to jerk him back and down. Joe lost his balance and fell into his brother, sending them both crashing to the ground.

Freed from the bonds that had kept it doubled over, the top of the young sapling whipped up from the ground. The force of the sudden release pushed the small tree almost all the way in the other direction. The top branches whacked Joe's face before the tree snapped back. It whipsawed violently a few times before settling back into its normal upright stance.

When the tree stopped shimmying, Joe got a good look at what he had almost walked into. The stake was long enough to puncture his chest, punch a hole in his back, and leave enough of the point sticking out to do some serious damage to anyone close behind him.

"If every car came with one of those gadgets," Joe remarked as he got up, "auto theft rates would go way down."

"Watch every step you take," Frank cautioned. "There could be more."

"I don't get it," Joe said. "Why would the Assassins set this trap for us?"

"That's not too hard to figure out," Frank replied. "They never really intended to let us join up with them. They were just using you to get at the Gray Man."

"That's possible," Joe admitted. "But why bother going to all this trouble to kill a couple of insignificant teenagers? We don't even know how to find them. We don't know their names. If that pilot's real name is Bob, my real name is Carbunkle."

"This booby trap is real," Frank countered, tapping the sharp stake. "If the Assassins didn't leave this little surprise for us, who did?"

"Somebody who doesn't like us?" Joe ventured.

"Good guess," Frank said. "Could we narrow that down a little?"

Joe thought about it for a minute and nodded. "An Assassin who doesn't like us."

"You think one of the terrorists did this on his own? Who?"

"If I had to bet on it," Joe replied, "I'd put my money on Boris."

No other surprises jumped out to greet them as they worked their way slowly to the Jeep. There was a large manila envelope resting on the driver's seat, and Joe was itching to find out what was inside.

"Don't touch anything!" Frank snapped, slapping Joe's hand away as he started to reach into the Jeep for the envelope.

Frank leaned into the cab and scrutinized the dashboard, seats, and floor. He popped the hood release, moved around to the front of the vehicle, and ran his fingers along the grille on both sides of the safety latch before thumbing the latch to lift the hood. He inched the hood up a crack and peered under it. Then he lifted the hood all the way and went over the engine like a wary used car buyer. After that he got down on his hands and knees and checked underneath the Jeep.

When Frank was finally satisfied that the vehicle wasn't going to blow up the first time he sneezed, he picked up the envelope from the front seat and opened it.

"Boom!" Joe blared in his brother's ear, cupping his hands around his mouth.

Frank dropped the envelope and staggered back. His eyes narrowed to an icy glare when he saw the wide smirk on his brother's face. "That wasn't funny," he said.

Joe scooped up the envelope and shook out the contents. "One map and one set of car keys," he noted. He hopped into the driver's seat, stuck the key in the ignition, and started the engine. "Let's go for a ride."

A great deal less eagerly, Frank climbed into the passenger seat. "We could be driving right into a trap, you know."

Joe shrugged and shifted into first gear. "When has that ever stopped us?"

"I'll say one thing for the Assassins," Joe said an hour later, shifting gears to take the Jeep down a steep grade, "they sure know how to map out a scenic route."

The gravel "highway" they were on wound down to a long bridge across a wide river.

There were mountains behind them, mountains to the right and left, and more mountains waiting ahead on the other side of the rushing river. The rough road that cut a swath through the evergreens was the only man-made scar on the pristine wilderness.

Under other circumstances Joe might have enjoyed the ride and the scenery, but now he couldn't stop thinking about Gina. It was hard to believe she was dead. He knew it wasn't his fault, but he still felt guilty because she'd died to save him.

Frank glanced over at the odometer and then checked the map. "We've been traveling north on this road a little over forty miles," he noted. "So that must be the Yukon River. Another hour at this rate and we'll be inside the Arctic Circle."

"Make it an hour and a half," Joe responded as the Jeep rumbled across the bridge. "There's a gas station and a restaurant up ahead. I want to stop to fill up the tank and my stomach."

"Sounds good," Frank said, turning into the restaurant's parking lot. "It's a long haul to the next town."

Once inside the restaurant they found a corner table and ordered lunch. Frank glanced around to make sure nobody was close enough to listen in, then leaned across the table and spoke to his brother in a low voice. "Our number-one priority should be to make sure the Assassins don't get the information they need to make the bomb."

"That's up to Dr. Stavrogin." Joe pointed out.

"Exactly," Frank said. "So we have to contact Stavrogin as soon as we hook up with the Assassins and get him out of this mess."

The whispered discussion was interrupted by the arrival of their food, delivered by a jovial, round waitress. "Are you boys up here on vacation?" she asked.

"That's right," Frank responded.

"We always wanted to see the Arctic Ocean," Joe added.

"That's too bad," the waitress said, "because you can't get to the ocean on this road."

Joe frowned. "What do you mean? The Dalton Highway goes all the way to Prudhoe Bay, doesn't it?"

"Sure it does," the waitress said. "But you need a special permit to drive past Disaster Creek. That's about a hundred and fifty miles from here."

Frank pulled the map out of his pocket, pushed the dishes out the way, and unfolded the map on the table. "Could you show us where that is?"

The waitress leaned over and studied the map. "It's not marked, but it's right about here." Her finger rested on a spot about an inch below an *X* penciled on the map.

"We have a small problem," Frank told Joe after the waitress had drifted off to refill coffee cups. "The place where we're supposed to rendezvous with the Assassins is about fifty miles beyond the point where we can go legally."

"No problem," Joe said with a smile. "I'll get us the first three-quarters of the way there. All you have to do is come up with a plan to get us the last twenty-five percent of the distance."

Frank didn't need to work out the numbers in his head. "You mean you'll drive the hundred and fifty miles to Disaster Creek, and I have to figure out how to get us onto the restricted highway past there."

Joe didn't respond. He just continued to smile through a mouth full of food.

As it turned out, Frank and Joe got lucky. Verna, the waitress, introduced them to a trucker who was on his way to Prudhoe Bay to deliver supplies for the Alaska Pipeline. He had a big truck, a light load, and a permit to drive past Disaster Creek. Thinking that the Hardys were just a couple of tourists in a tough predicament, he agreed to smuggle them and their Jeep in the trailer of his truck.

Many hours later when they were safely out of sight of the Disaster Creek checkpoint, the trucker swung open the wide double doors of the trailer and pulled out the ramp. After thanking the trucker, Joe drove the Jeep back out onto the road.

The country grew more rugged as the Hardys drove north. They gradually climbed higher into the foothills of a jagged, snow-capped mountain range that stretched across the horizon.

"We're heading into the Brooks Range," Frank informed his brother. He checked the map again. "We're also pretty close to the spot marked on the map."

"There's a side road coming up on the left," Joe observed.

"Turn off there," Frank said. "Let's see if it's where we're supposed to go."

The side road soon narrowed to a rough trail and finally dead-ended in a twisted, rocky gully, which was blocked by a jumble of boulders. Joe got out of the Jeep to investigate. There was no way the Jeep could get over the wall of rocks that choked the narrow passage, and the sides of the gully were too steep for the Jeep to climb.

"Looks like we'll have to ba—"

Joe's words were cut off by a sudden movement overhead. A wide shadow fell over the Jeep. Joe jerked his head up and saw something huge hurtling down on him. As it slammed into him, he thought he heard a coarse, vicious laugh above him.

Chapter
14

THE HEAVY WEIGHT smashed into Joe, forcing him to his knees. But it was hardly the bone-crushing impact of a massive boulder, which was what he'd guessed the object to be. Instead, it was some kind of ropy net, with oddly shaped patches of grayish green fabric attached to it and small tree branches lashed to it here and there.

Joe crawled and clawed his way out from under the thing. When he looked at the net sprawled across the gully, covering the entire Jeep, he finally realized that it was camouflage netting, the kind the Assassins used to hide their helicopter. A shape rippled under the net, and Joe remembered that his brother was still under there. "Frank!" he called out, lifting a corner of the net. "Are you okay?"

"I'll live," Frank responded as he struggled free of the ropy web.

Harsh laughter echoed down into the gully. Frank and Joe both raised their heads at the same time.

"You!" Joe yelled, pointing an accusing finger at the curly-haired terrorist standing on the rim of the steep gully.

"You will have to learn to be more alert if you want to become Assassins!" the man shouted down.

"And you'll have to learn to be a better driver if you want to make it as a cabbie!" Joe shot back. "Is this your way of getting even because we didn't tip you after you took us sightseeing at the bottom of the Potomac?"

The man laughed again. "Put some rocks on top of the netting to hold it down, and make sure the Jeep is completely covered."

"What if we don't?" Joe responded defiantly.

The Assassin waved a stubby submachine gun at them. "Then I will shoot you. If you cannot follow simple orders, you are useless to us."

Frank and Joe shared a brief glance. "Just shut up and do what the man says," Frank said in a low voice.

The Hardys quickly secured the camouflage netting with heavy rocks at each corner. Up close it looked like a net with some junk stuck on it draped over a Jeep. From a distance Joe knew it would melt into the background, taking on the appearance of a thousand other lumpy patches of brush.

"All right, that's good enough!" the curly haired man called down. "Now get up here!"

Frank and Joe scrambled up the side of the gully. At the top another spectacular view greeted them. Grass and moss and rocks sloped down into a small, bowl-shaped alpine valley. In the distance the brooding, snow-capped spires of the Brooks Range pierced the sky.

The curly-haired Assassin picked up a small backpack and slung it over one shoulder. The camouflage pattern on the backpack matched the swirls and blotches of white and gray on the man's pants and jacket. Frank had been too distracted by the view to take note of the terrorist's outfit before. But as soon as he did, he instantly knew what the stark colors meant. The Assassin was wearing winter camouflage, and in the high mountains it was winter all the time.

"Let's go," the man said. He turned and

trudged down the gentle slope toward the pond.

"Where are we going?" Joe asked.

"Not far," the Assassin responded vaguely.

As they hiked down into the small valley and worked their way around the pond to a level, grassy area, Frank had a question for their cabbie. "Why did you go into the Potomac with us? You could have been killed."

"I was supposed to bail out before we went over, but I couldn't get my door open." The curly-haired man then dropped the backpack and sat down on a large, rounded rock.

"Are we taking a break already?" Joe asked doubtfully.

"We're waiting," the man answered.

"Waiting for what?" Joe prodded.

"You'll see," the man said.

Joe sighed. "You're real spellbinding in the art of conversation. Do you have a name?"

The Assassin smiled. "You can call me Bill."

"I'm starting to see a pattern emerge," Joe remarked. "Bob, Boris, Bill . . . What if our names don't start with the letter *B?*"

The man shrugged. "Your old names are not important. You will be given new ones."

While Joe was trying to pump the terrorist for information, Frank sat scanning the sky.

He spotted the distant helicopter before he heard the rhythmic *whup whup whup* of its whirling rotor blades.

The chopper swooped into the valley and touched down on the grass. Bill ran over to the cargo door, yanked it open, and jumped in. Frank and Joe climbed in after him, and the chopper lifted off as the curly-haired terrorist slammed the cargo door shut.

"Where are we going?" Joe asked again.

"Into the mountains," Frank told him.

"How do you know that?" the familiar voice of Bob called out from the pilot's seat.

"Simple observation," Frank replied. "Winter camouflage means there's a lot of snow where we're going. The only place with snow within helicopter range is on the mountains."

The pilot nodded thoughtfully. "Very good. I like a man with a keen eye. You will make a good Assassin if you prove yourself worthy—as your friend has done."

Frank didn't like the sound of that. Joe's entrance exam to join the terrorist group had been to kill the Gray Man. The Hardys had managed to fake that one with the help of the intended victim and some jerry-rigged special effects. If the Assassins expected Frank to kill someone, too, he had severe doubts that he and Joe could pull off a similar stunt again and without help.

Frank started to shiver but not from fright. He was cold. The helicopter wasn't built for comfort. As it climbed higher into the mountains and the temperature dropped, the cargo bay turned into a refrigerator. He wouldn't complain, and he knew Joe wouldn't, either. They had to be tough if they wanted the Assassins to accept them, and Joe was an expert at playing tough.

Peering between the pilot's and copilot's seats, Frank looked at the view beyond the curved windshield. Bob was skirting the edge of a bulging glacier and threading the chopper through a narrow, snowy pass with huge slabs of bare rock thrusting up on both sides. Heavy winds buffeted the metal bird, and more than once Frank was sure it was going to careen into one of the towering walls of granite.

Beyond the pass were more craggy, snow-capped mountain peaks. Frank thought he saw wisps of smoke rising from one of the peaks, but it was probably just blowing snow, swirling in the crosswinds. As the helicopter neared the jagged mountain teeth, Frank spotted a ledge on one of the peaks. At the back of the ledge was a wide-mouthed cave.

The pilot steered the helicopter toward the

ledge. Now Frank could see a few figures moving around in the front of the cave, and he knew this had to be their destination.

After a bumpy landing on the windswept mountain shelf, Frank and Joe helped lash down the helicopter's landing skids. They covered the bird with a large white camouflage tarp that they tied to steel stakes driven into the solid rock.

Frank's hands were numb by the time they finished. He and Joe followed the pilot into the cavern mouth, which turned out to be a shallow cave. A number of crates were stacked up on one side of the cave, and a jumble of camping gear was piled up next to them.

Three tunnels fed into the cave. The pilot led the Hardys down the left-hand tunnel. Like the Assassins' other hideout in the mine shaft, the tunnel was lit by bare electric bulbs strung from the ceiling and powered by portable generators. Unlike the mine, however, Frank couldn't always stand upright in the tunnel. There were a lot of places where they had to stoop down or hunch over.

Frank noted a few other important differences, too. First, there were no timbers shoring up the tunnel. So it was a natural tunnel, not one dug by men and machines. Second, the sides were bumpy but not rough. In fact, the surface was as smooth as glass in some places. Third, the tunnel was definitely getting warmer as they moved farther down the passage.

Frank remembered the wisps of smoke he had seen from the helicopter. Not smoke, he corrected himself—steam.

"Lava tube," he said out loud as the answer hit him.

Joe glanced back over his shoulder at his brother. "What did you say?"

"Lava tube," Frank repeated. "This tunnel was created by hot lava flowing out of a volcano. We're inside an extinct volcano."

The pilot stopped and turned around. "Not quite extinct," he said.

Frank frowned. "I didn't know there were any active volcanoes this far north in the interior of Alaska."

A slight smile appeared on the Assassin's lips. "There weren't." He started walking again. "Watch your step," he cautioned. "The footing gets a little tricky up ahead."

The tunnel angled down sharply, and the pilot braced his hands against the walls as he worked his way down the steep passage. Frank and Joe followed his example. After a few twists and turns, the lava tube fed into a wide, deep cavern.

Frank couldn't tell how big or high it was

because the only light came from inside two tents pitched on the floor of the cavern. In the dim orange glow that filtered through the thin nylon walls, Frank could see a large bearded man standing guard outside one of the tents.

Joe saw him, too. "Say, Bob," he said to the pilot. "Did you know that somebody left us a little present to go with the Jeep?"

"Present?" Bob echoed. "What are you talking about?"

Joe described the booby trap that had almost skewered him.

The pilot chuckled. "It's not a very reliable method, but it's one of Boris's favorites. He does not approve of my decision to recruit you.

"Boris is entitled to his opinion, of course," he continued with a smile. "But discipline must be maintained."

The pilot strolled over to Boris, said something Joe couldn't make out, and then, without warning, slammed his fist into the bearded terrorist's stomach. Boris doubled over. The pilot grabbed his hair, yanked his head back, and spoke a few more words in his cool, casual tone, never raising his voice and smiling his inhuman smile the whole time.

"Boris is deeply sorry for his irresponsible actions," the pilot told the Hardys. "I will

Survival Run

consider appropriate punishment when this mission is completed. Right now we all have important work to do.''

''Does that include us?'' Joe asked.

''Of course it does,'' Bob responded. He nodded toward the tent Boris had been guarding. ''Dr. Stavrogin is in there. You are to guard him until I return. You can take turns on watch. The other tent has cots and sleeping bags.''

''What about guns?'' Joe ventured.

The pilot continued to smile. ''I don't think you'll need them just yet. I'm sure the two of you are strong enough to handle Stavrogin until Krinski verifies his equations. Then we can dispose of the old man.''

Frank stared at the pilot. ''You mean, kill him?''

The Assassin met Frank's gaze with his cold, unblinking eyes. ''Exactly. And *you* will be his executioner.''

133

Chapter

15

FRANK HAD SEEN this coming. He'd known he would have to prove himself to the Assassins. These guys were killers. If you wanted to join the group, you had to be a killer, too. So telling him to kill Dr. Stavrogin would be a simple, logical test in the twisted minds of the terrorists.

Before the two Assassins, Bob and Boris, reached the lava tube that led out of the cave, Frank's brain was working overtime. From what Bob had said, Stavrogin might have already divulged the formula that the terrorists had been trying to pry out of him. But with luck the Hardys might be able to save the physicist and stop the Assassins before they could use the information to build a hydrogen bomb.

A plan was forming in Frank's mind.

As soon as Bob and Boris were out of sight, Frank turned to his brother. "We have to work fast," he said in an urgent whisper. "The first thing we have to do is find out what Stavrogin told the Assassins."

They went into the tent and found the physicist sleeping fitfully on a cot. Joe woke him gently and introduced him to Frank.

"We're going to get you out of here," Frank told Stavrogin.

"It's too late," the physicist said glumly. "They know everything now. Somehow, they found out that I have a sister in Russia, and they even know where she lives. When they discovered that the equations I had given them were worthless, they threatened to kill her if I didn't give them the real formula."

He shook his head wearily. "I was so tired. They didn't let me sleep for days." He looked up at the Hardys with great pain. "What have I done?"

"You did what you had to do," Frank said softly. "Do you know anything about somebody named Krinski?"

"I only know that he is some kind of scientist and that he knows enough about my work to detect faulty equations," Stavrogin replied. "I gather that he is working with the Assassins."

"Is he here, somewhere in this complex of tunnels and caves?" Frank asked.

"I don't think so," Stavrogin said. "Several times I overheard them talking about sending the equations to him. I got the impression that he wasn't even in Alaska."

That complicated the situation but simplified the options from Frank's point of view. If Stavrogin's formula hadn't gone beyond the secret mountain base, the Hardys could activate the hidden transmitter and bring a small army of Network agents down on the Assassins' lair. If Stavrogin was right, though, then the critical information was already in the hands of terrorists in an unknown location. A Network strike now might only spur them to double their efforts and produce a bomb on a much shorter timetable.

The plan that had been cooking in Frank's brain since he found out he was to be Stavrogin's executioner was definitely starting to look like the only real option available. He could see that the physicist was a little on the old side, and more than a little worn down by his ordeal. Frank just needed the right props to pull it off.

"This may sound a bit weird," Frank said

to the physicist, "but do you have any experience with hang gliders or parachutes or anything like that?"

Stavrogin's face brightened a little. "I was a paratrooper in the Russian army. I haven't jumped in years, but I'm still in good shape. I jog three miles a day when I'm home."

"That's good," Frank said, "because you're going to need all your strength and parachute training for this to work."

Joe stared at his brother. "What's the plan?"

"You stay here with Dr. Stavrogin," Frank said. "We're supposed to be guarding him, so stand outside and look like a guard."

"And what are you going to do?" Joe asked.

"Find a hang glider," Frank answered.

"Gee, that might be a little tough," Joe remarked. "The nearest store that carries hang gliders is probably two thousand miles from here."

Frank shrugged. "Then I'll just have to make do with whatever I can find."

Frank's first stop was the other tent in the cave. There were two cots with sleeping bags inside it. He also spotted a couple of heavy winter parkas. They didn't need the parkas in the cave, but Frank made a mental note to come back for one of them later.

Next, he had to get back to the first cave, the one that opened onto the mountain ledge. As Frank hiked up the lava tube, he heard a muffled rumble from somewhere far beneath him, and a faint tremor ran through the tunnel. He thought about the strange warmth inside the mountain and Bob's cryptic comment regarding active volcanoes. There was only one logical conclusion. The Assassins had brought the extinct volcano back to life. But how—and why?

Frank's train of thought was cut off by the sound of voices nearby. The air was cooler here, and he realized he was near the end of the lava tube. The voices were coming from the entrance cave. He waited and listened. The voices faded away. They had probably gone down one of the other two tunnels.

Frank moved forward again and cautiously stepped out into the entrance cave. It was empty except for the crates and supplies haphazardly stacked against one wall. Frank went through the pile of discarded equipment quickly. He knew exactly what he was looking for, and he soon found it buried under a portable camp stove. In fact, he found two and decided to take them both.

He carried the gear back down the tunnel

to the cave where his brother and the physicist were waiting, dropped the two sacks on the ground, opened them, and spread the contents on the cavern floor.

Joe stared at the array of poles and nylon fabric. "Terrific. Two more tents. Just what we needed. Now we can each have our own and still have one left over for a visitor." He looked at his brother. "I thought you were going to get a hang glider."

"I did," Frank said. "You just can't see it yet. All the raw materials are right here. What is a hang glider, anyway? A bunch of poles, some rigging, and a big sheet of sturdy, lightweight nylon. Now, what do we have here?"

Joe looked at the assorted tent parts and realized that the essential components of a tent and a hang glider were basically the same. But he could also see that it would take major surgery to transform the tent parts into a working hang glider. "Do you really think we can do it?" he asked doubtfully.

"We don't have a choice," Frank replied grimly. "This is our only chance."

"But we don't have any tools," Joe pointed out.

Frank dug into his pants pocket and fished out his Swiss army knife. "We have this."

* * *

When Frank decided the glider was as good as they could make it, he folded it up, grabbed one of the parkas out of the tent, and hauled them both back up the tunnel. He prayed he wouldn't run into any of the Assassins. If they caught him now, he knew he wouldn't be able to explain away the crude flying rig.

There were more ominous rumblings from deep inside the mountain that made the ancient lava tube tremble. Frank didn't let that slow him down. The faster he got outside, the lower the risk that he'd be discovered.

When he reached the end of the tunnel, he checked the cave entrance to make sure it was empty, then dashed across it and out onto the windy, bitter-cold mountainside ledge. The sun hung low in the southern sky. This far north, Frank knew, the sun never really set in midsummer. That was good because Stavrogin's chances would be slim enough without having to steer the jerry-rigged hang glider through the mountains in the dark.

Frank stashed the glider and the parka under the camouflage tarp that covered the helicopter, then hurried back down his tunnel. When he got back to the inner cave, one of the terrorists was there waiting for him.

"Ah, there you are," Joe said as Frank came out of the tunnel. "I was just telling

Boris that you went looking for the bathroom. Did you find it?"

"I didn't know you two spoke the same language," Frank replied.

"Boris speaks English," Joe said. "Not well, but you can kind of understand what he's saying. Just before you got here, he was telling me how he was going to carve his initials in my face if I didn't tell him where you were. I understood that pretty well."

"Well, I'm here now," Frank said. "What's up?"

The bearded Assassin's dark gaze shifted between the two brothers. "It is time," he said in a thick accent.

"Time for what?" Frank responded. He already knew the answer but didn't know if he was ready to face it.

The brooding Assassin pulled a .45 automatic pistol out of his shoulder holster and handed it to Frank. "Time for you to become one of us. Time to kill the old man."

Chapter

16

FRANK TOOK the pistol from the Assassin. It felt heavy in his hand. He knew he couldn't shoot Dr. Stavrogin, but the gun might be useful if anything went wrong.

Then he remembered one of the fundamental rules his father had taught him about firearms: Never pick up a gun if you don't intend to use it. He gripped the pistol by the barrel and handed it back to Boris.

"I won't need this," Frank said.

The bearded Assassin's dark eyes narrowed. "You refuse to carry out the execution?" he growled in his heavy accent.

"I didn't say that," Frank replied. "I said I won't need the gun. There are much more interesting ways to kill a man, don't you think?"

Boris raised his eyebrows. "Oh?"

Frank nodded. "Remember those flying lessons you wanted to give us?"

A thin, savage smile curled the corners of the Assassin's mouth.

"I thought you would," Frank said. "Why don't we take the old man outside, push him off the cliff, and see how well he flies? That way we won't waste any bullets, and we won't have a body to get rid of.

The terrorist let out a cruel, harsh laugh. "That is a fine idea. You will make a good Assassin." He ducked into the tent and dragged Dr. Stavrogin out. "Come, old man. Time to go."

Stavrogin blinked and looked at Frank. "Where are we going?"

Boris laughed again and roughly pushed the physicist toward the tunnel. "You will find out soon enough."

Frank leaned over to his brother and whispered in his ear. "Stay close to our bearded buddy."

"Why?" Joe asked.

"Because you're going to accidentally trip and fall into him," Frank said.

Joe glanced at his brother. "I am?"

Frank nodded. "And it's going to be a really nasty fall, too."

"It is? How nasty?"

"So nasty Boris won't make it to the end of the tunnel."

"That's pretty nasty," Joe whispered with a slight smile.

Something roared in the depths of the mountain, and a violent tremor shook the cavern. Frank and Joe reached out and steadied each other.

"This neighborhood is getting dangerous," Joe remarked. "It used to be such a nice, quiet place. Do you have any idea what's going on?"

"I think the Assassins woke up a sleeping giant," Frank responded. "And I don't think the giant is happy about it."

Frank didn't know what the terrorists hoped to accomplish by bringing the volcano back to life. The pent-up forces churning in the magma beneath the earth's crust could easily obliterate the top half of the mountain in an explosive burst far more devastating than the most powerful nuclear weapon.

The Hardys followed the Assassin into the tunnel. Frank edged past Boris and get between him and Stavrogin.

"Keep moving!" Frank snapped, giving the

physicist a light shove. Stavrogin jerked his head around, obviously confused. Frank winked at him and gave him another nudge. He had to put some distance between them and the "accident" that was about to happen. He hoped the physicist would understand that the rough treatment was only an act to fool the terrorist.

Joe's part in the act turned out to be fairly easy. A distant blast echoed up the lava tube, followed by a tremor that rippled along the passageway. Instead of putting his arms out to brace himself against the wall, Joe rolled with the shock wave and added a little force of his own as he hurled himself at his target.

"Whoa!" Joe cried out for effect as he smashed into Boris's back. The Assassin grunted and pitched forward as Joe clutched the man's arms and threw all his weight against him. With his arms pinned to his sides, Boris couldn't use his hands to break his fall. He toppled over and his head smacked hard against the rock floor.

Frank pulled his brother off the Assassin, then bent down close to the man's head. Blood trickled from a gash in Boris's forehead. He moaned softly, but his eyes were closed and he didn't move.

"He's out cold," Frank said to his brother.

"You stay here with him. If he comes out of it, stall him as long as you can."

Joe nodded. "Don't worry about Boris. I can handle him." He reached out with his right arm and shook hands with Dr. Stavrogin. "Good luck," he said with a smile. He knew the physicist would need a large dose of luck to get off the mountain alive.

Frank led Dr. Stavrogin out to the ledge on the mountainside. The bulk of the covered helicopter concealed them from anybody who might wander out through the entrance cave.

Stavrogin put on the bulky down parka while Frank lashed together the last pieces of the hang glider.

"I'm sorry we couldn't test it," Frank said as he strapped the physicist into the harness. "Do you know how to use a hang glider?"

Stavrogin's eyes darted over the contraption, and he nodded. "The aerodynamic principles are simple enough." His gaze shifted to Frank. "Do not concern yourself with me. You have given me a chance and hope, which is far more than I had before. Now you must forget about me and do everything you can to stop these madmen."

"We'll stop them or die trying," Frank assured him. He checked the rigging one more time to make sure all the lines were secure.

"One last thing," he said, reaching down and taking off his shoe. He dug out the tiny homing device. "I don't know how far you'll get in the hang glider, but I know you won't get far enough to walk out of these mountains on your own. When you land, turn on this little gadget. It shouldn't take long for friends to find you after that."

Frank showed the white-haired physicist how the homing device worked and then handed it to him.

"I cannot thank you enough," Stavrogin said.

"Don't thank me yet," Frank replied with a faint smile. "We don't even know if the thing works."

Stavrogin shrugged. "We will never know until we try it. I am ready."

Frank helped him to the end of the ledge. "Well, this is it, I guess," Frank said.

"Yes, it is," Stavrogin responded, and before Frank could say anything else, the physicist leapt off the ledge.

Frank gasped as the hang glider plunged down a hundred feet or more, then caught an updraft and soared away. Frank watched it intently, holding his breath, waiting to see if the flimsy device would fall apart and plummet out of the sky. When nothing happened

147

after a few minutes and the glider was just an orange speck in the distance, he began to think Stavrogin had a real chance.

Then he remembered the physicist's parting words and hurried back into the cave.

A series of powerful underground explosions rocked the mountain as Frank ran down the tunnel toward the spot where he had left Joe and Boris. The Assassin was awake and on his feet when Frank got there. Frank assured the groggy terrorist that he had gotten rid of Dr. Stavrogin, which was basically the truth.

"I think we'd better get out of here," Joe said as the lava tube shuddered from the force of another subterranean blast. A section of the solid rock ceiling collapsed behind them, choking the tunnel with dust and debris.

"Good idea," Frank agreed quickly. "Let's head back to the entrance cave. I have a bad feeling this mountain is about to blow its lid, and I don't think Bob is going to hang around to watch the fireworks."

A half dozen men poured out of the other two tunnels at the same time the Hardys did. The pilot and the curly-haired Assassin were already yanking the white tarp off the helicopter.

"Ah, good!" the pilot shouted when he saw

Frank and Joe. "I was afraid we might have to leave you behind. This phase of the project has been a great success. Now we move on to the final stage. You are lucky to have joined us on the verge of our greatest triumph!"

"Sounds exciting," Joe said, trying to sound like an eager recruit as the terrorists crowded into the helicopter. "What exactly is the final stage?"

"You will find out soon enough," the pilot responded as he started the engine and the rotor blades began to spin overhead. "For now, let us just say that we will change the world forever."

Frank and Joe exchanged a troubled glance. They both knew that any change the Assassins were planning wasn't likely to benefit anybody else living on the planet.

Ten hours later, bone-tired from being awake almost constantly for the past two days, Frank and Joe were back in the airport in Fairbanks. They were sitting in the departure lounge, waiting for a plane.

"I still don't get it," Joe said, stifling a yawn. "I can understand why the Assassins would put us on a commercial flight. Even though they might have a few helicopters, they probably don't have a fleet of intercontinental jets. But I still don't understand why they're letting us travel alone."

"It could be another test," Frank suggested. "For all we know, one of the other passengers is an Assassin assigned to keep an eye on us."

"Two of them, actually," a voice murmured from the seat behind him.

Frank fought the urge to turn to face the man. "Mr. Gray?" he whispered.

"Yes," the Gray Man said, "although you'd never recognize me."

Joe vaguely recalled that a nun had been sitting there a few minutes earlier.

"You'll be happy to know we found Dr. Stavrogin," the Gray Man continued. "He broke his leg and a couple of ribs when he landed, but he should be fine in a few months. That was quite a job you boys did with that hang glider."

"How did you find *us?*" Frank asked.

"As soon as we picked up the signal from the homing device, we rerouted an air force surveillance jet to scan the area. We tracked a low-flying chopper that hadn't filed a flight plan and figured you might be on it. We've had somebody on your tail ever since."

"Do you have any idea why the Assassins are shipping us off to Hawaii?" Joe asked.

"If I did," the Gray Man answered, "I probably wouldn't let you go." He paused for a moment, then said, "You can still back out if you want."

"No, we can't," Frank said grimly. "Stopping the Assassins is more important than whatever might happen to us."

"And we owe it to Gina," Joe added.

The Gray Man sighed heavily. "I hate asking you boys to take on this dangerous job, but you're the best chance we have to stop the Assassins. We know they have Stavrogin's formula, and if Krinski really is work—"

"Krinski?" Joe cut in. "The Assassins mentioned that name."

"Yes, I know," the Gray Man said. "Stavrogin told us. That's why I'm letting you get on a plane to Hawaii instead of one back home to New York. If Krinski is involved, the situation could be much worse than I originally anticipated. We have to move fast, and a couple of inside men are our best shot."

Joe wondered what could be worse than a hydrogen bomb in the hands of a bunch of bloodthirsty terrorists.

"By the way," the Gray Man added, "you might be interested to know that Alaska has a new volcano. There was a huge eruption in the Brooks Range this morning, not too far from where we picked up Stavrogin."

"Looks like the Assassins' little experiment backfired on them," Joe said.

"I wouldn't be so sure about that," the Gray Man responded ominously.

"Attention, passengers," a pleasant, relaxed woman's voice announced over the intercom. "Flight Five-sixteen to Anchorage is now boarding at Gate Twelve."

Frank glanced at his ticket. "That's us. From Anchorage we take a nonstop flight to Honolulu." He looked over at his brother. "I'm ready. How about you?"

Joe nodded and stood up. "I'm with you— all the way."

Frank smiled and put an arm around his brother. "As long as we stick together, nothing can stop us."

Concluding the Ring
of Evil Trilogy:

From Atlanta to Alaska to the exotic shores of Indonesia, Frank and Joe Hardy have penetrated the inner sanctum of a worldwide terrorist network: the Assassins. Now, drawn into the enemy's lair, the Hardys face their greatest challenge and greatest risk—to uncover the true purpose and power of the violent criminal conspiracy.

Trapped deep in the Indonesian jungle, their covers blown, the boys can't afford to turn back. They confront a force so potent, and an intelligence so evil, that there's no time to seek reinforcements. Braving the heights of terror, Frank and Joe alone will have to defuse an explosive scheme that could erupt into a catastrophe of global proportions . . . in *The Pacific Conspiracy,* Case #78 in The Hardy Boys Casefiles™.

Most Archway Paperbacks are available at special quantity discounts for bulk purchases for sales promotions, premiums or fund raising. Special books or book excerpts can also be created to fit specific needs.

For details write the office of the Vice President of Special Markets, Pocket Books, 1230 Avenue of the Americas, New York, New York 10020.

SUPER HIGH TECH ... SUPER HIGH SPEED ... SUPER HIGH STAKES!

VICTOR APPLETON

He's daring, he's resourceful, he's cool under fire. He's Tom Swift, the brilliant teen inventor racing toward the edge of high-tech adventure.

Tom has his own lab, his own robots, his own high-tech playground at Swift Enterprises, a fabulous research lab in California where every new invention is an invitation to excitement and danger.

☐ TOM SWIFT 1 THE BLACK DRAGON ....67723-X/$2.95
☐ TOM SWIFT 2 THE NEGATIVE ZONE ....67824-8/$2.95
☐ TOM SWIFT 3 CYBORG KICKBOXER ....67825-6/$2.95
☐ TOM SWIFT 4 THE DNA DISASTER ....67826-4/$2.95
☐ TOM SWIFT 5 MONSTER MACHINE ....67827-2/$2.99
☐ TOM SWIFT 6 AQUATECH WARRIORS ....67828-0/$2.99
☐ TOM SWIFT 7 MOONSTALKER ....75645-1/$2.99
☐ TOM SWIFT 8 THE MICROBOTS ....75651-6/$2.99
☐ TOM SWIFT 9 FIRE BIKER ....75652-4/$2.99
☐ TOM SWIFT 10 MIND GAMES ....75654-0/$2.99
☐ TOM SWIFT 11 MUTANT BEACH ....75657-5/$2.99
☐ TOM SWIFT 12 DEATH QUAKE ....79529-5/$2.99
☐ TOM SWIFT 13 QUANTUM FORCE ....79530-9/$2.99

    HARDY BOYS/TOM SWIFT ULTRA THRILLERS:
☐ TIME BOMB ....75661-3/$3.75
☐ THE ALIEN FACTOR ....79532-5/$3.99

Simon & Schuster Mail Order
200 Old Tappan Rd., Old Tappan, N.J. 07675
Please send me the books I have checked above. I am enclosing $_____(please add $0.75 to cover the postage and handling for each order. Please add appropriate sales tax). Send check or money order–no cash or C.O.D.'s please. Allow up to six weeks for delivery. For purchase over $10.00 you may use VISA: card number, expiration date and customer signature must be included.

Name _____

Address _____

City _____ State/Zip _____

VISA Card # _____ Exp. Date _____

Signature _____

788

NANCY DREW® AND THE HARDY BOYS®
TEAM UP FOR MORE MYSTERY... MORE THRILLS...AND MORE EXCITEMENT THAN EVER BEFORE!

A NANCY DREW AND HARDY BOYS SUPERMYSTERY
by Carolyn Keene

In the NANCY DREW AND HARDY BOYS SuperMystery, Nancy's unique sleuthing and Frank and Joe's hi-tech action-packed approach make for a dynamic combination you won't want to miss!

- ☐ DOUBLE CROSSING   74616-2/$3.99
- ☐ A CRIME FOR CHRISTMAS   74617-0/$3.99
- ☐ SHOCK WAVES   74393-7/$3.99
- ☐ DANGEROUS GAMES   74108-X/$3.99
- ☐ THE LAST RESORT   67461-7/$3.99
- ☐ THE PARIS CONNECTION   74675-8/$3.99
- ☐ BURIED IN TIME   67463-3/$3.99
- ☐ MYSTERY TRAIN   67464-1/$3.99
- ☐ BEST OF ENEMIES   67465-X/$3.99
- ☐ HIGH SURVIVAL   67466-8/$3.99
- ☐ NEW YEAR'S EVIL   67467-6/$3.99
- ☐ TOUR OF DANGER   67468-4/$3.99
- ☐ SPIES AND LIES   73125-4/$3.99
- ☐ TROPIC OF FEAR   73126-2/$3.99
- ☐ COURTING DISASTER   78168-5/$3.99
- ☐ HITS AND MISSES   78169-3/$3.99

Simon & Schuster Mail Order
200 Old Tappan Rd., Old Tappan, N.J. 07675

Please send me the books I have checked above. I am enclosing $_____ (please add $0.75 to cover the postage and handling for each order. Please add appropriate sales tax). Send check or money order–no cash or C.O.D.'s please. Allow up to six weeks for delivery. For purchase over $10.00 you may use VISA: card number, expiration date and customer signature must be included.

Name _____

Address _____

City _____ State/Zip _____

VISA Card # _____ Exp.Date _____

Signature _____ 664-03

EAU CLAIRE DISTRICT LIBRARY

THE HARDY BOYS® CASE FILES

☐ #1: DEAD ON TARGET	73992-1/$3.75	☐ #48: ROCK 'N' REVENGE	70033-2/$3.50
☐ #2: EVIL, INC.	73668-X/$3.75	☐ #49: DIRTY DEEDS	70046-4/$3.50
☐ #3: CULT OF CRIME	68726-3/$3.75	☐ #50: POWER PLAY	70047-2/$3.50
☐ #4: THE LAZARUS PLOT	73995-6/$3.75	☐ #52: UNCIVIL WAR	70049-9/$3.50
☐ #5: EDGE OF DESTRUCTION	73669-8/$3.50	☐ #53: WEB OF HORROR	73089-4/$3.50
☐ #6: THE CROWNING OF TERROR	73670-1/$3.50	☐ #54: DEEP TROUBLE	73090-8/$3.50
		☐ #55: BEYOND THE LAW	73091-6/$3.50
☐ #7: DEATHGAME	73993-8/$3.99	☐ #56: HEIGHT OF DANGER	73092-4/$3.50
☐ #8: SEE NO EVIL	73673-6/$3.50	☐ #57: TERROR ON TRACK	73093-2/$3.99
☐ #9: THE GENIUS THIEVES	73767-4/$3.50	☐ #58: SPIKED!	73094-0/$3.50
☐ #10: HOSTAGES OF HATE	69579-7/$2.95	☐ #60: DEADFALL	73096-7/$3.75
☐ #11: BROTHER AGAINST BROTHER	74391-0/$3.50	☐ #61: GRAVE DANGER	73097-5/$3.75
		☐ #62: FINAL GAMBIT	73098-3/$3.75
☐ #12: PERFECT GETAWAY	73675-2/$3.50	☐ #63: COLD SWEAT	73099-1/$3.75
☐ #13: THE BORGIA DAGGER	73676-0/$3.50	☐ #64: ENDANGERED SPECIES	73100-9/$3.75
☐ #14: TOO MANY TRAITORS	73677-9/$3.50	☐ #65: NO MERCY	73101-7/$3.75
☐ #29: THICK AS THIEVES	74663-4/$3.50	☐ #66: THE PHOENIX EQUATION	73102-5/$3.75
☐ #30: THE DEADLIEST DARE	74613-8/$3.50	☐ #67: LETHAL CARGO	73103-0/$3.75
☐ #32: BLOOD MONEY	74665-0/$3.50	☐ #68: ROUGH RIDING	73104-1/$3.75
☐ #33: COLLISION COURSE	74666-9/$3.50	☐ #69: MAYHEM IN MOTION	73105-X/$3.75
☐ #35: THE DEAD SEASON	74105-5/$3.50	☐ #70: RIGGED FOR REVENGE	73106-8/$3.75
☐ #37: DANGER ZONE	73751-1/$3.75	☐ #71: REAL HORROR	73107-6/$3.75
☐ #41: HIGHWAY ROBBERY	70038-3/$3.75	☐ #72: SCREAMERS	73108-4/$3.75
☐ #42: THE LAST LAUGH	74614-6/$3.50	☐ #73: BAD RAP	73109-2/$3.99
☐ #44: CASTLE FEAR	74615-4/$3.75	☐ #74: ROAD PIRATES	73110-6/$3.99
☐ #45: IN SELF-DEFENSE	70042-1/$3.75	☐ #75: NO WAY OUT	73111-4/$3.99
☐ #46: FOUL PLAY	70043-X/$3.75	☐ #76: TAGGED FOR TERROR	73112-2/$3.99
☐ #47: FLIGHT INTO DANGER	70044-8/$3.75	☐ #77: SURVIVAL RUN	79461-2/$3.99

Available From Archway Paperbacks
Published By Pocket Books

Simon & Schuster Mail Order
200 Old Tappan Rd., Old Tappan, N.J. 07675

Please send me the books I have checked above. I am enclosing $_____ (please add $0.75 to cover the postage and handling for each order. Please add appropriate sales tax). Send check or money order—no cash or C.O.D.'s please. Allow up to six weeks for delivery. For purchase over $10.00 you may use VISA: card number, expiration date and customer signature must be included.

Name _____

Address _____

City _____ State/Zip _____

VISA Card # _____ Exp.Date _____

Signature _____

762-02